THE PALACE

After a few months of surviving on pretty small, not overly compelling jobs, I received a commission in my inbox. A medium-scale installation to commemorate the 750-year anniversary of a former palace, now a historic house open to the public. I would later learn that no one had actually ascertained whether this anniversary marked the laying of the first foundation, the day it welcomed its first inhabitants, or the first time it appeared in local records. When a site badly needs a cash injection it is incredible how irrelevant such details can become; a significant date is chosen, special events are put on, footfall increases. Sometimes the brief visibility afforded by marketing means film or TV scouts will stop by and be enchanted by the well-appointed rooms and breathtaking gardens. A block booking of a month or two, a significant fee. Then it is not a palace with a history, but the location of filming for such and such, and people come for tours, filling the café and gift shop. The email didn't say these things explicitly, but in these places – unless the roof is about to cave in – money tends to be spent only with the anticipation of making more back. Feed the horse a sugar lump and hope it shits out a nugget of gold.

~

I have been deciphering archives and curating semi-permanent scenes (domestic, culinary and otherwise) in medieval buildings for the past twenty-two years. When you see a replica feast scene in the great hall of an old building, I am the person who placed the pomegranates beside the pie, and for a very good reason. When you come upon a room, cordoned off with red rope, beyond which you see an open book on a desk, a chunk of bread picked hollow, and a quill in an ink pot that is empty of ink, I am telling you something about the person who lives in that room. The ink may be purple, and even though no one can see it in the straight-forward sense, one in a thousand people will sense it. Ultimately, I want my work to communicate with everyone, but it is those people I really hold in my mind.

MAY WE FEED THE KING

MAY WE
FEED THE KING

Rebecca Perry

GRANTA

Granta Publications, 12 Addison Avenue, London W11 4QR

First published in Great Britain by Granta Books, 2026

A CIP catalogue record for this book is available from the British Library.

1 3 5 7 9 10 8 6 4 2

ISBN 978 1 80351 386 7 (hardback)
ISBN 978 1 80351 388 1 (ebook)

Typeset in Arno Pro by Iram Allam

Printed and bound by CPI Group (UK) Ltd, Croydon, CR0 4YY

The manufacturer's authorised representative in the EU
for product safety is Authorised Rep Compliance Ltd,
71 Lower Baggot Street, Dublin D02 P593, Ireland.
www.arccompliance.com

www.granta.com

For Ross

I

WE HAVE LONG
ADMIRED YOUR WORK

The head office staff wanted six scenes in specified locations – the King's chambers, the kitchens, the Queen's parlour, an Attendant's quarters, something that showcased the medical paraphernalia and practices of the time (in a location deemed most appropriate by me once I knew the site) and a feast scene in the great hall. They also asked whether I would consider, for an additional fee, taking part in some activity on the anniversary weekend itself. I would have some part to play in shaping what that looked like, but they envisioned a 'Meet the Experts' day on the Saturday, during which members of the public could visit me, along with other experts, naturally, and ask anything they liked. They also wondered about a short, informal talk on the Sunday, to coincide with some media activity.

I would think about it, I told them, and give an answer as soon as possible.

As commissions go the requirements were clear, not too restrict-
ive. The fee and budget for materials were decent. The house also
had its own records, which were kept on site – detailed ledgers of
the Kings and Queens who once resided within, and accounts of
the habits and customs of the court. Archives of this kind are near
enough unheard of.

~

At this point, certain things had happened in my life. I was ready
to immerse myself.

ORDER AND DISCREPANCIES

There is a website dedicated to the provision of plastic replica food to people like myself, as well as to other professional curators, purveyors of historical re-enactments, drama teachers, amateur dramatics groups, showrooms (kitchens, furniture, etc.) and so on. The index starts with 'barbeque', then 'biscuits and cereals', followed by 'bread', 'cakes, gateaux and meringues', running through to 'fruit', 'historical foods', 'vegetables – prepared'.

Almost anything you can imagine, or at least could feasibly need.

I know this website back to front, can navigate its pages like a map I barely need consult. I could tell you, for example, that the gherkins are with the celebration food and not the vegetables, that a rustic loaf is in historical foods but nowhere to be found in the bread section.

The delicatessen section offers six pages of various cured meats, sausages and pies. A pork joint covered in muslin is £45, yet a single parma ham slice costs £14. A half oyster shell, the exposed flesh shining as if with the freshest brine, is £31.25 for a single piece; but a full, cooked, vividly red leg of venison is not much more, at £55. These discrepancies in price are often baffling and unexplained, but, I trust, justified; it is my opinion that we should never presume to know the intricacies of another person's craft. The pork joint is a particularly interesting piece, the muslin itself also being a replica and completely rigid, yet still appearing as if brusquely wrapped by capable hands mere moments before: one illusion inside another.

The dairy section is a heaven of creams and whites, cheeses and butters portioned into squares and pats and rounds. Emmental in not-waxes of red and yellow. The Camembert is the best of the cheeses, slightly trumping the Edam for attention to detail with its tactile powdery skin.

Apple green. Apple red. This page bursts with primary colour. Just £3 each; a fruit bowl made cheaply.

There is the most beautiful ham slice, with a pollen-like bread-crumbed perimeter. Slices of white lard curling almost impercept-ibly at the edges, as if cut and left on the side to dehydrate.

The new potatoes (boiled) look like nothing more than beige lumps, overly shiny – disappointing, given the utter lack of complexity of a potato – but the small potatoes (unwashed) are so faithful you can almost feel the fine grit of them in your mouth.

~

The chicken leg (whole, cooked) is one of the few items I consider flawless. It is, unlike so many other items, perfect for those rare installations with no barriers or ropes, in which the items and the viewer will be in thrillingly close proximity. Once, quite without warning and close to the deadline, the dwelling of a witch-hunter was added to a large-scale commission I was working on at a living museum. I crammed his desk full of well-burnt candles to show that this was a man with zealous commitment to his work, and that he'd pore over evidence in the dead of night like a wolf over a pile of bones. I wanted the windows spotless, the curtains always pulled aside. The rats remained cowering in the corner, not daring to approach, so chilling was his aura. The reins for his horse hung by the door next to a worn-out whip. But the food – the little I would allow him – I put off thinking about until the last moment, because I knew I had no choice. The budget was spent by then, and all I had available in my stock to suit the time period was the whole chicken leg. Every fibre of my being cried out against giving it, this perfect meal, to this man. But in the circumstances there was no alternative – he had to eat.

~

The website's artichokes lack adequately defined scaliness – they are altogether slightly too smooth – but they have real spirit to them. From a distance they pass, but they would never survive scrutiny. In some cases, this is no bad thing. It all rests on the context.

The beef tomato – 'low in stock' (i.e. discontinued) – is a joke and may as well be a squeezy ketchup bottle. This I know without having seen one in the flesh. I have wondered in the past about writing to the supplier about this particular item, which in my opinion is so crass that it risks letting down their entire outfit. This is something I would have been more inclined to action a few years ago, before my great lesson in perspective.

The chewet – a small meat pie – appears so real you could pick it up and take a bite – I actually sniffed the first order I received. Even now, when manipulating its position in a scene, I step back to observe its new placement and find I am smelling the hand that just touched it, quite without realising.

There are nine options for replica eggs. They include the coveted double yolk (fried), a neatly folded golden omelette and a perfect whole fresh brown egg. A poached egg, with a cloudy film of white across the yolk, looks perfectly done (£15). This is possibly my favourite page, glowing yellow like a farmhouse kitchen. Perhaps not coincidentally, my relationship to eggs, of all the foods, has been most affected by my work. What I mean by this is that they are the only item for which the replica has eclipsed the real thing, which I now handle in a cavalier manner. I expect brown eggs to bounce. After cracking the shell, I often anticipate that the yolk and albumen will slip out white, flat, already fried. The desire to penetrate the white belly of a poached egg on a friend's plate with my finger is often close to irresistible. But it does not yet fully overwhelm me – when it does, I will take it as a sign that I have lost my grip.

The herb section is scantly stocked and the greens dim, but I would never use replica herbs in my work anyway, when real ones add such scent to a room. I have yet to experience a soundscape which truly brings life to a space; when you can unquestionably hear the clanking of pots and the cleaving of bone, the cook shouting for more flour, your brain is not compelled to fill those gaps. But scent – scent is depth, and depth is a dark pool we may dive into.

I often deploy the 'fresh herb' test to gauge the success of a scene I have created. It is thus: if the herbs betray that the replica food is an illusion, it is a failure, and I start again.

~

As for spices, people might think historic diets consisted only of cloves and maybe black pepper, but the reality is that the rich had access to pretty much anything. Ginger, cinnamon, saffron, bay and anise were hugely popular, the food richly spiced, the recipes elaborate and complex.

More than once, doing the rounds of historic buildings of particular importance or interest to me, I have observed what could have been a breathtakingly elaborate kitchen scene dressed with no more than some potatoes, a slab of meat and a pile of vegetables, as if the wealthy lived like the poor. This is what happens when people don't call in the professionals.

MY GREAT LESSON
IN PERSPECTIVE

Around three years ago, while visiting a stunning property, I observed on the periphery of a distinctly mediocre kitchen-table scene three grey plastic fish lying perfectly parallel to one another in a rectangular ceramic dish. The fish looked like something from the chew-toy aisle of a pet store – one-coloured, a seam visible at the belly, their fins not distinct entities but part of the same mould as the body. Their eyes were utterly dead, but not as eyes which had once held life. I waited until the room was empty, then I removed the fish and walked away with them in my bag. This was during what I now think of as my past life – towards the end of it, in fact. And I can admit that the bluntness of this solution reflects something of my state at that time. My situation, the pain of it, was something I had no choice but to exist within. But the fish, how unacceptable they were in the scene, *that* I could do something about. So, I curated. Back at home, I took the fish out of my bag, observed them lying lifeless on my bed, and put them away in a drawer. I uncovered them some weeks later and moved them again, to a less visited cupboard. But the fact of their presence in the house persisted, like a low hum. Eventually I gifted them to the child of a friend – they were disproportionately huge in their play kitchen, and the friend seemed somewhat horrified by the scale of them, but the child was delighted.

ALL WORK IS HOLY

I work to one guiding rule when I create my scenes. Within this rule are contained all the others pertaining to colour and balance and space. It applies whether I am working on a table scene for two littered with small hints of intimacy – food and drinks and cutlery left askew – or on a bedroom scene, with its focus on linens and tucked coarse bedding, the careful placement of materials for ablutions. It's the same for a huge feast scene with metres of spilling platters; the same for the cell of a monk who owns nothing but the clothes on his back, a holy book and the meagre stub of a candle.

The rule is this: it must appear as if the person or people have just left the room. The viewer must feel as if the air is alive with their energy, that they only just missed them, that they will be back at any moment. If this isn't the case, the scene is no more than an arrangement of objects. The scene is dead.

PEEKING THROUGH A CRACK
IN THE CURTAIN AND SEEING
ANOTHER CURTAIN

When trying to make sense of what I do, people sometimes say to me, *Did you want to be a painter?*

No I didn't, is always my reply.

~

People also ask me why I do it – a line of questioning which naturally follows when I have confirmed that the calling is not a particularly lucrative one, nor in overwhelming demand.

I suspect that to pick too much at the scab of the question would be to kill the magic, so I tend, at this point, to squirm my way out of the conversation. I ask them why they do what they do, as if it is equally reasonable to levy this line of questioning at a city worker, knowing their answer will be predictably unsatisfying, knowing that the unsayable answer is money.

But what I *do* know, and rarely tell people in conversation – conversation being as it so often is the death of imagination – is that creating these scenes fills me with a feeling unlike any other.

I remember the first time this happened.

Browsing for sofas with my parents in a furniture superstore on a weekend – I must have been six or seven years old – I came upon a living-room scene with a three-piece suite, a standing lamp and a coffee table upon which was placed a television remote and a bowl full of plastic grapes. I approached the bowl, squeezed a single grape flat, and watched it expand back to its original grape shape. I don't remember the colour of the sofa, how soft or hard it was, whether the TV was large and impressive, what we ate for lunch that day, whether my parents told me off for anything I did, if there was rain, snow, sun, distress, treats, or clouds with no sky between them. I remember seeing the fruit bowl, reaching out for the grape to confirm its fakery, not caring that it didn't become pulp between my fingers. Preferring that it didn't.

In that moment, I was overcome by the sensation that I was in someone's living room, in their life. That they would enter, demand to know who I was and what the hell I thought I was doing there. Their eyes would burn with panic, which would settle into something closer to a desperate questioning – a questioning I could not satisfy, being as I was a vision manifested in a place and time out of my control.

I was transported – I loved it.

~

Do you think a part of you wants to escape your own reality?

This question has been levelled at me more than once, always by people who believe themselves particularly insightful or who, if you ask me, would be better off spending their energy asking themselves the same thing. My response is often withering. This is something I'm aware of and that I have tried, as I age, to control.

When my circumstances changed, and it became plain to those around me that I was floundering, my work served as a kind of conversational solace. *Tell me what you're working on,* people would say when it dawned on them that the questions had run out, and there was no other comfort to offer. In this way, my work has sustained me when people could not.

IF YOU LOVE SOMETHING

The difficult thing about what I do – and it is the only drawback I have unearthed in more than two decades – is that when my scenes are ready, when they are perfect, I have to accept that I cannot control how people interact with them.

Some examples:

- **Cleaners jostling the items.** In-depth cleaning of the scenes – if they are to remain in situ for extended periods of time – is to be undertaken by me and me alone. Me and my special cloths. I am very clear about this, but the message rarely reaches those who need to hear it. I don't blame the cleaners for this – it is simply that people do not take my request seriously enough to pass it on to them. Or they think I won't notice.

- **Members of the public stepping beyond the rope to get a closer look.** My scenes are designed with a specific viewing distance and angle in mind, tailored to the doorway, window or cordon they are being observed from. The illusion is shattered so easily when someone sets their own parameters by sneaking past a NO ENTRY sign, unclipping a rope, or moving into a different light. I believe you can tell a lot about a person who doesn't believe the rules apply to them, but that is another thing entirely.

- **Actors in costume interacting with the scene.** I once witnessed a jester use three replica pomegranates to demonstrate his juggling abilities. The weight – or the lack thereof – of the fruits took him by surprise and he fumbled one almost immediately. It bounced hollowly on the majestic parquet and rolled under the feasting table, eventually nudging the toe of a shoe of a visitor, for whom the illusion was shattered. Worse, an utterly crass King – in the middle of a hammy speech about a typical day in his life – freed a large chicken leg from a meat platter, sending the other joints and chops scattering, and held it aloft as he boomed on and on. Then, the prop finished with, he placed it gingerly back on the table, upside down, where it sat with the fakery of its flat bottom and manufacturer's logo exposed to the crowd.

THE ROOM WITH GLASS EYES

Back to the palace celebrating its unspecified 750-year anniversary. I visited the venue during a normal Monday when it was open to the public.

Someone showed me to the room that I would be working from. It was a beautiful space – all original flooring and beams, hanging tapestries on the walls which had retained their colour remarkably. Along the left-hand wall, an impressive desk sat in front of the largest window, bathed in light. The back wall, to my right, was cluttered with many stacked chairs, a dehumidifier and various props and displays for school visits. A life-size cardboard cut-out of a knight in armour imploring, 'Guess how much my chainmail weighs!' A kitchen worker, hands in apron pockets, declaring, 'The court eats 250kg of mutton a day!' An attendant, staff in hand, confiding, 'It is my job to guard the King's bedchamber at night.' Straight ahead of me, punctuating the space between the desk and this paraphernalia, were six windows, portals to the gardens.

The person who'd brought me to the room handed me a single door key and left me to settle in, telling me someone would return in half an hour to give me a tour. I was free to leave anything I liked in the room. The archivist would be on site the next morning and had made their day free for me. This courtesy did not go unappreciated.

I set my bag on the table and circled the room, pausing at each window to look down on the gardens. They were vast, divided into sections that dated back to the palace's most recent renovation some five hundred years ago. In the foreground, rectangular hedging encased the flower beds, which congregated around the central fountain. A block of shrubbery divided these ornamental gardens from the potager garden, itself punctuated by high arches. Nothing but green to see at this time of year, but beautiful nonetheless, and perfectly symmetrical. The final window overlooked the maze which – in line with the fashions of the time – I could presume obscured an aviary. There were perhaps forty people navigating the maze's walkways – in constant motion, not unlike bees in a hive. I watched them until I heard a knock at my door. Two volunteer guides, prompt and cheerful, had arrived to fetch me for the tour. They wore matching T-shirts, mid-blue like a school uniform.

One of them was newer than the other, who had given her time freely to the house for fifteen years and knew its every shadow and fold. Where her eyes scanned every inch of the place, reaching for details and facts and interesting stories that caused her to glow as she relayed them to me, the newer team member lacked any palpable sense of connection to the rooms and grounds. They were remarkably similar in appearance, but the fervour of one compared with the dispassion of the other rendered them as a silk rose in bloom and a paper carnation, its green stem wrapped around twisted wire.

STAY BEHIND ROPE AT ALL TIMES

I asked to first be shown the cellar and buttery. Starting in the windowless bowels and moving up through the building gives me the feeling of being a scuba diver slowly rising for air. I was then taken to the kitchens, pantry and larder. *Will you want to see the storerooms?* they asked. *Of course*, I replied.

The pace of the tour was a little too fast, so I slowed my walking slightly and the guides fell in line.

We walked through the royal bedchambers, extensive quarters for the nobility granted permission to reside at court, the great hall, its antechambers, up and down narrow staircases and through further corridors, sub-rooms, the council chamber, the garderobe, and on.

We ended in the palace gardens, beside the large pond.

You've never had scenes arranged here before? I asked. The experienced one replied that there used to be a few, but they were done by the volunteers, so they were pretty basic and everyone felt they were cheapening the rooms. I agreed: *In that case, better to have nothing at all.*

At this point, before I had begun my work in earnest, the tour had a purely practical function. I noted each twist and turn, each room in relation to at least two other rooms so that I wouldn't need to be escorted again. It was what I call a 'blank tour', in which I didn't allow the rooms to speak to me, or permit myself to notice any small shifts in the air.

Did I have any questions, they asked. I did not.

CONSIDERATION

After my tour had finished, I walked the palace corridors alone, passing through rooms but not loitering. I noted when the air grew lighter and denser, where the chills sat, sensing its bloody corners. When light caught a certain window, or moved in a beam across a hallway, I would marvel, before wondering how many others had done so before me. I acquainted myself with the many portraits, allowed myself to enter into a dialogue with some of them. I inspected the tapestries, found their imperfections, imagined hands working. I ran my fingers over carvings in doors and panels.

I touched stone so cold it seemed wet, wood as soft and warm as melted wax.

~

One room in the servants' quarters, both in its dimensions and in its atmosphere, though not at all in its appearance, took me back to the first commission I accepted after my life as I knew it had ceased to exist. I was only weeks into the devastation of it, but still

I had to work. The tiny rooms in an almshouse needed to be recreated as if for the nuns who would once have lived there. They had slept, prayed, committed scripture to heart, wept, all in their one room. Each room would be different, of course, as we people are, but when you are representing lives which were dictated by order, obedience, humility and the forgoing of earthly pleasures, there is only so far you can go.

I arrived and entered the first dwelling, the one furthest from the communal dining hall, and therefore the most modest. It was completely empty, the white stone walls and silver-grey flagstone floor giving it the feeling of being inside a shell.

In that room, I arranged a small wooden table centrally and added a white tablecloth, one well-worn wooden chair and a very low stool. A plate of replica bread (small, tough-looking rolls), an open book (uses for common herbs), a closed Bible (palm-sized, leather-bound), a pewter cup with a handle. A wooden walking stick, a ladder leading to the upper level – more a nook than a mezzanine – which consisted of a narrow bed a foot or so below the ceiling. I hung a bushel of dried sage on the wall.

It wasn't a huge amount of work. Nonetheless, when everything was in place in that first room, I was exhausted. In the weeks preceding that commission, every decision and every movement had drained me to empty. Now, I wanted nothing more than to stay in that room for a day and a night, to mirror the nun's movements, to inhabit her entirely. To understand how she might have woken, eaten, bathed, prayed, talked, taken herself to bed. To better know if she craved wine or sex; whether you can crave something you've never had. As her, I imagined, my brain could be empty of its loud poison, my heart filled with nothing but simple devotion to a God I would be absolutely sure existed. As her, I would not even allow myself a second to question my life, my mousehole of a room.

I asked if I might sleep there, overnight, just once. The young project manager looked at me with humour, assuming it was a joke, then with pity, confusion. She said she would ask. She walked away fast, returned quickly. It was, regretfully, a no. She blamed the terms of the insurance.

~

Teasing out life in a dead space, though possible, is akin to making an animal from a folded paper napkin.

But the palace was teeming with life – it spoke to me, and I would speak back.

WHITE GLOVES

The next morning – a fresh day, like cutting into an apple. I drove to the palace, keen to swim once again through its chambers.

The archivist was waiting in a dim room. They always are. The better to protect the fragile pages, but, I suspect, they enjoy the drama of it too – their white gloves glowing as they beckon you inside, like a mystic bidding you come observe your future in a pale fire. I have levelled this suspicion at many an archivist over the years, and they have always reddened and appeared taken aback. On this occasion, however, I did not feel compelled to comment. There had been a second, upon entering, when I saw the archivist before they noticed me. Something in their face told me that this was a person to be taken seriously. It was without question.

Welcome, they said, and pulled a chair out for me. I thanked them for making the time. The archivist said it is always a pleasure to meet a curator, especially one bothering to take an interest in the history of the specific building. They asked me what I would like to see.

What is there? I asked.

Everything, came the response.

I felt my heart in my chest. I felt light with anticipation in a way I hadn't for some time. Two years? Maybe three? How long had it been?

Everything meant: a detailed ledger which recounted the reign of each king and queen for the past half-millennium, as well as some records from the early Middle Ages; recipes spanning at least the same time period; detailed accounts of feasts, celebrations, coronations. The utter tedium of accounts and coffers and debts – hundreds upon hundreds of pages of them. Medicinal and botanical remedies, plans for the gardens, letters from foreign rulers and dignitaries. Prayers and poems and songs. Detailed instructions for fixing roofs, ridding the kitchens of pests, cladding a building damaged by storm.

The archivist said that the ledgers of the Kings and Queens read like a relentless catalogue of praise – sometimes insipid, rarely believable. More like reading about legends or saints than real people.

But there are a couple of notable exceptions, they said.

~

We were at the table, our heads bent as if to drink from this pool of knowledge, for almost two hours.

It was too much. I said so.

The archivist suggested we break for lunch. We could get a discount in the café – the food was good, fresh. I assured them I needed no looking after, that I could fend for myself, and excused myself to return to my room, needing space to order my thoughts.

POINT OF FUSION

I have a recurring dream:

I am in the courtyard of a seafood restaurant in a coastal town. It is an actual restaurant that I know and once ate in with friends. During this meal, one friend cracked the claw of a lobster and her face and chest were covered in a white spray, like paint. She sat frozen, with her eyes closed for a few seconds, steeling herself for the eventuality of the moment when she must observe the damage.

In my dream, the courtyard is empty, save for one person who sits alone at a small circular table. The person has an empty white plate in front of them, upon which I place two oysters (unshucked). The oysters have a good weight to them. One sits neatly between two pressed palms; it is gnarly, with a shell of numerous greys. There is a completely convincing line where the two halves meet, where the knife goes. I have never in real life found a replica to match it.

When I have placed the oysters on the person's plate, I ask them, *Why did you order the oysters? Are they a treat?*

And they say, *My friend has died and oysters were their favourite thing to eat in the sun, and I always refused to try one because I was worried I would have an allergic reaction or choke and make a scene somewhere nice. And I hate the look of them, I really hate the look of them. But now I'm trying to honour my friend by being brave, or letting them know that they were right, I should absolutely try something that so many people say is delicious. And my friend would always say 'Come on! What's the worst that can happen?'*

I ask them how their friend died and they say, *I don't really want to think about it if that's OK.*

The person stares down at the oysters. They say, *The longer I sit here the more upsetting it seems to be doing this without them. As if I've waited for them to die before listening to them. Like, how contrary does that seem? And they've been in the sun for maybe ten minutes now, which can't be good?*

I ask if I should take the oysters away. The person replies, *No. What do you think? Should I just eat them now that they're here? Would it be a nice gesture . . . like an act of memorial?*

I say that their friend won't know about it either way. These words come out with a cruel edge to them, though I believe I had meant them as a sort of comfort.

The person begins to tear up, their eyes glinting in the sunlight of the courtyard.

NOT ALL SEEDS NEED
LIGHT TO GERMINATE

The archivist knocked at my closed door. I called out for them to come in, somewhat resenting the interruption.

They wanted to ask about my process. They couldn't resist. Did I have half an hour for them? *Maybe five minutes*, I said.

How did I begin? What parameters, if any, did I set myself? To what extent was I prone to working on feeling? Did I ever let it get the better of me? What did I see my role as being for the viewer? Where did auteur meet artist meet curator, if at all? What did I *want*?

I gave my answers as best I could, and each time I found the follow-up question to be not what I expected, but precisely what I wanted. Five minutes became half an hour, then more. I hardly noticed.

Start with recipes, the archivist suggested, *and the more detailed accounts of meals taken and feasts held. I can extract them for you. Ignore the people, for now.*

Did I resent being given direction in this way? Instinctively, a little. But I knew it was logical – utterly logical.

CHECKOUT

There's something that can happen when I am embarking on a project on the scale of the work at the palace, and so heavily focused on food scenes: my appetite sours, and real food becomes something of a threat. I can't be sure if it is becoming more or less real, too much itself, too vivid, or something altogether different. Whatever, it makes me not want to eat.

For example, the evening that I returned home from my very first day at the palace:

I was buying something for dinner, but I didn't know what; I was circling the aisles waiting for something to feel ingestible.

I picked up a whole chicken, which I could roast and eat for three or four meals, then use the carcass for soup. If I could not enjoy it, I rationalised that it might as well be economical.

After placing the chicken in the basket, my hand felt tacky. I brought it to my nose and didn't like what I could smell – brine and blood. I opened and closed my fist multiple times, testing the stickiness.

I bought tomatoes, mushrooms and fresh ginger, coffee, biscuits and soy sauce, pinching the items with my fingers, not wanting the chicken juice on the rest of my shopping. I lifted a bunch of bananas from the display – the skin had split on one of the fruits, down its stomach. I returned the bunch immediately, fearing what might now be inside. Something crunchy, surely, and with legs, living in a tight convoy down the centre.

Queuing for the checkouts, I looked at a baby sleeping in the pram in front of me. Their parent had placed a vacuum-packed rack of ribs at the baby's bare feet, and held bread, detergent and a bunch of mixed flowers in their arms. The ribs' red juices beneath the plastic formed a network of lines which overlaid the purple thread veins of the meat, pulled thin over the bone, and rested on the baby's leg – plump and creased – as if wanting to merge with it.

I felt compelled to place my hand gently on the arm of the parent and say, *Please move that meat away from your baby – or something bad will happen.*

~

Back at home, I couldn't face the chicken. It had the pallor of something sickly that had never seen the light. I found space for it in the freezer, then put the kettle on to boil water for pasta, and chopped onions, garlic and celery. Fried them in oil. Salted it. Added anchovies and regretted the salting. Left the pasta water plain. I couldn't imagine tolerating a flavour other than salt so I held back from adding anything else, cooking the pasta and stirring it through with the colourless sauce. Once deposited in the bowl, I concealed it with parmesan and black pepper.

Each evening, the moment I turn off the extractor fan and the kitchen light and walk past the table where we used to sit and over to the sofa – those few seconds are the quietest of my day. I can hear my own breathing inside my nose and throat. I walk quickly, take the most direct route, and I turn on the TV immediately.

THEY EXPECTED I WOULD THROW THIS TOGETHER

I spent some days reading copied pages from the ledger – refreshed frequently by the archivist, who appeared in the room out of nowhere, silently leaning over my shoulder and placing a new sheet on the desk. *You'll like this*, they'd say. *You'll want to see this.* I tried not to invite too much conversation, but their sudden presence at my shoulder sent a sensation through my torso and chest, like missing a step.

A couple of times a member of the office staff popped their head around the door and enquired, very casually, whether I might be starting to assemble the scenes that day or the next day. Just so they could cordon off the room I would be working in and get signage ready to divert the public. I assured them that I understood their nervousness, but that I would meet their deadline, that this was always my process. I was lying.

Typically, I spend a day or two reading whatever records are available, ensuring I have a clear time period for the scene(s) in my mind. A common misconception is that I will be utterly fixated on historical accuracy; the truth is I find it stifling. I would never do anything egregious, of course, but it is much more important to me that I know the key information of the characters I am dealing with – like, this dinner scene is a replica of the meal taken by seven traitors the night before they planned to carry out their meticulously laid plot to murder their King at his breakfast table. So, I can assume that they knew there was a not inconsiderable chance they would die (they did) and that they would therefore have eaten the best, the rarest, food that would have been available to them. They would have drunk wine, good wine, but not too much. Then, because I know that their plot was foiled (of course it was), and that they were in fact arrested at that very table, mid-meal, tender meats still in their mouths, I would consider the manner in which the plates and goblets would have been left. How to convey the surprise, the very early onset of panic, perhaps a guard arrogantly quaffing the last of their wine in front of them and sending the empty vessel clattering across the table before they were escorted from the room.

But there, at the palace, I found myself in an entirely different situation. Drowning in details. No, not drowning – luxuriating.

~

To placate the office staff, I told them I would be happy to take part in the weekend of activities celebrating the palace's anniversary. *And I wondered if I might make a suggestion? I thought the archivist and I could join forces on the Saturday – also, perhaps you might dim the room, and set display cabinets of manuscripts, segments of tapestry and pinned-open books around the perimeter.* For the love of God, I thought, give the place some atmosphere. Expecting people to walk freely into a silent room, brightly lit, to converse with a lone human – and not just any lone human, but one that deep down they suspect might enjoy making them feel stupid – is ludicrous. I've been there before. People panic. It must be the two of us together, rousing lighting and low music, with things to look at. Then may come conversation.

EXCAVATION, ON MY
KNEES IN A DITCH

I found my King on the fifth day.

The archivist had entered the room, placed a thick pile of papers at my elbow and said, *I think that's it for entries about food – now we move on to the people.*

I found his scant entry in the ledger almost immediately – it was in my hands, as if I had manifested it, with no knowledge of what came before. The single page dedicated to his reign was now a mess, with marginalia and footnotes added over time as his story retrospectively evolved – was altered, challenged, embellished, struck through, left to rest as one great question mark by people who damned him.

It's important to say that I cried, I wept, when I saw it.

What a reduction of a life.

~

To relay the King's ledger entry in its fullness would be to undo everything I set out to achieve in my conjuring of his person. And so I refuse it.

~

The Apple King (also referred to as the Traitor King) would have been an interesting choice. Peril, sadness and tragedy. But his entry in the ledger gave me no sense of the man beyond that of a terrible coward, and what an injustice to present someone in such a way. No colour or context, no texture, and therefore no dignity.

I rarely opt for Great Rulers, for the monarchs famed for abundance – the resulting scenes can be generic and overly fussy. Where is the personality, the nuance, in a table piled with every conceivable roast meat, pastry, pudding and fruit? What real good can come from presenting to the public the preferences and tastes of people who willingly, joyously, have a great shoe on the neck of their people? People who can have everything and so do. We know them well enough already. But – for example – a small silver fish head on a plate, placed on the floor for a cat? That gives us a sense of a person, and begins to animate a room. A discarded sheet taking on the shape of a ghost.

~

The archivist had approached me once or twice over the preceding days, keen, I sensed, for conversation about my progress. I had been too preoccupied for any meaningful interaction, but now, having discovered my King, I found I needed to locate them. They were in the office making photocopies, chatting to a guide. I asked if they would come with me to my room when they could – ideally immediately. We left the office together, and once I had closed the door to my room behind us, they asked what I had found.

I gestured to the King's entry, resting like a fallen leaf on my desk. *Do you know him?*

I do.

He'll be the one, I said.

They placed a hand on the entry. *Of course.*

SHEEP GRAZING AFTER A STORM

On the Saturday, I somewhat reluctantly took a day away from the archives to visit a gallery with a friend. I enjoy the freedom of moving around with a companion, speaking openly, but not having to maintain eye contact over a table or at awkward angles on a sofa. We talked about what had happened in our lives in the three or so months since we'd last caught up, chatting quietly and easily, stopping in front of paintings that drew us in. She was well, as were her children, but she complained about work, the onset of some hip pain. She asked me how I was, really and truly, and she placed her hand on my arm. What she meant was how was I getting on being alone in the house, reshaping my life? She said she knew that people tend to stop asking after a few months, maybe a year, and that can make a person feel ashamed if they are still suffering. She said this in front of a fairly gloomy pastoral scene, with thick white blobs of sheep, and a brilliant smear of yellow-white indicating a break in the clouds.

I was better, I said, things were changing.

CIRCLE CASTING

My King began as a loosely held rendering. Like a distant memory of a person I once met. But once the archivist had isolated other court records from the time we knew to coincide with his reign, my eye was able to isolate anything pertaining to him, and it jumped out of the text like a spark. A commission to the embroiderer, a tally of the kitchen's dry store, a request to the head gardener.

He and his Queen brought with them a complexity befitting a project of this scale. They also helped to situate the scenes in an approximate period. This was useful for no other reason than to serve as a helpful mental boundary for me, dictating the availability of certain ingredients, reflecting the culinary fads of the time, and enabling me to visualise my cast – their clothing, their hairstyles, the games they play, even their manner of walking. These boundaries are mine and mine alone.

I had found him, and now came the serious work of building his world around him.

TRADE ROUTES

That second week, I started taking the photocopies home with me in the evenings when I left work. I read them on the train and bus – if I drove, I placed them on the passenger seat, with the King's ledger entry at the top of the pile. Though I still struggled to eat, I sometimes found myself able to sit at the dining table in my house, the papers spread around me like a mosaic. The empty chair at the table, the one opposite, felt like a chair again – simply vacant, and not a void.

~

One evening on the way home from the palace – after a full day in the shadow of the archives, where we had sat, the archivist and I, my left biceps pressed against their right, making a double-width human – I stopped in a local bar for a glass of wine.

These are things that I had forgotten how to do, that I had forgotten were possible.

The bar was quiet and dark, with tealights bobbing in holders which were the reds, yellows and blues of stained glass. I was reading a translated letter from the archives, written by a visitor to court during the reign of my King. The writer speaks of their business – that of importing spices – and how it progresses. He speaks of the cold, the food, the miserable, sunken faces of the servants, the over-firmness of his bed, his surprise at the existence of the squirrel, the small red creature with its brush tail twitching in ecstasy against the blue sky. He makes only one mention of the King: he saw him once, walking through the main salon at court, and he looked like a man, just as any other, but quite lost. The archivist told me that 'lost' was the most faithful approximation of the word used in the original language, but nothing could capture it completely. The translator had explained their dilemma at the time, considering 'adrift' the only viable alternative, but unable to justify the connotations with water. As I read, a member of the bar staff – in fact, the only member – asked if they could clear my glass away, asked if I would like another one. When they returned with my drink, they asked what I was reading, so I told them about the palace, the archives, the ledger entry, the King, his court, my commission. When they replied that it was really beautiful for someone to be so in love with their work, I realised it was the only time anyone had ever said that to me. Others had noted how important it was to me, or that I took it so seriously, but not that I loved it.

~

Before I packed up that day, the archivist had told me that they could always eat penne pomodoro, even if they felt queasy. In thinking of it, I felt something resembling an appetite.

MADE MANIFEST

I began to dream of my King, first as a vapour misting the clarity of my usual nocturnal terrain – a flash of his cloak when I am a child lost at the beach, the sound of him clearing his throat as I attempt to run from an assailant in the street, in the rain, but remain fixed to the spot. Then, so vividly – my King and the world about him – that when I woke, briefly, to rearrange my position in bed, I felt his presence in the house. One night, I stirred in the usual and complete silence of my bedroom and heard, I could have sworn it, a scratching from the adjacent office – that of the King's quill at work.

~

The next evening, before nightfall, I sat in the quiet of my garden and watched two magpies gathering for their nest – one freeing twigs and the other pulling at the moss on the branches of the neighbour's birch.

~

My house had been holding its breath for a long time.

I DOST LOATHE TO WEEP

I sat on a bench with the archivist, on the lip of the ornamental gardens, surrounded by lavender. We had eaten our lunches, then split a flapjack from the café.

Did I want, they asked, to talk about the King?

After I had shown them his ledger entry in my room, and they had placed their hand on it in recognition, I had wept once again. This is not how I usually conduct myself, preferring to cry alone and briefly. The archivist didn't say *Don't cry*, or put an arm around my shoulders, or run out to get me a glass of water. They stood beside me waiting – I don't know for how long – then smiled when finally I looked up at them, and said to me, *It's good*.

I did not want to talk about the King, not then, so I said: *Not yet, but sometime soon, thank you.*

SHE IS ODD

Don't think I didn't notice the hardly casual glances in our direction. *Goodness me, the archives must be more extensive than we realised.* People were often whispering when the archivist and I exited a room.

I sensed I could delay no longer.

Eventually the most senior member of the palace staff challenged me directly about when my work would begin. They reminded me firmly of the deadline, said that it was fast approaching, as if I lack an understanding of how time works. I bit my tongue. I asked whether it would be possible to take some time alone in the house. I clarified that I meant without the public, knowing that no person – let alone a relative stranger to the place – would be afforded the honour of being truly unaccompanied. To placate him, I promised it would be the final step before I began assembling the scenes. That I had everything ready in my mind, all mapped out – it would all come together in a day – two, tops. He replied that I should stay late on Sunday. *The cleaners will be here for at least a couple of hours after closing, and will let you know before they lock up. I will also be in the office if you need anything.* He barely masked his frustration. While I can't say I blamed him for it, I did not care.

That night, I dreamt a slow and relentless dream in which eggs fell from my hands to the kitchen floor. On my knees, I made a hammock of my hands over and over again, scooping up the raw white and yolk, and then, just as my hands were clean and dry, another egg would fall at my feet.

ALL FIVE FINGERS

On the Sunday, the palace travelled gently towards silence as the public filtered out. It had been quiet anyway because of the sunshine – not a day for being inside a large, dark building.

The archivist and I leaned back against the front of the building, shoulders to the warm stone, arms folded. Willing people to leave.

When a steward confirmed that all the rooms were clear, I could begin my solo tour. The archivist accompanied me back inside, then took a sharp right for the stairs leading down to the archives.

I'll leave you to it, they said. *Take your time. Enjoy.*

Over the previous couple of days, wherever I stood in the building, I was aware of the archivist's glowing form in the basement below my feet.

I thought of the first time we had met – how they began to remove their gloves, one finger at a time, as they suggested lunch. I had almost thought they might bite and pull at them. That night, back home in the shower, I had recalled this vision and realised I had – briefly – stopped breathing.

EVERY ENTRY IS AN EXIT

Normally, when I am granted this kind of access to a place, I start in the kitchen. For me, of all the rooms, it is the easiest to animate – people in there tend to have their stations, turning the spit or cleaving the bones for stock.

I may run my hand over the indentations in the wood of a central table, and along the underside of the great open fire used for roasting meat. It might come away grubby, and when I smell it, it might smell of smoke and fat. I'll handle the tools – deep ladles of black metal, long silver forks, wooden spoons and spatulas – before testing the weight of the glazed pudding bowls and platters and returning them carefully to their places. I will stand beside a butchery block, lean my hip on its edge and close my eyes, listening for the rain on the roof and then the crackle of the fire creeping in, the sizzling fat of the pig, the squeak of the spit as it turns, the chatter, the shouts across the room, the chops, a persistent cough, the feet tapping a hectic rhythm on the floor, the clattering of platters and the thuds of full bowls placed on the large table by the door, ready for distribution. And above all else, the smell of meat: spitting its oil onto the flagstones; rising as steam and resting on the ceiling, where it will drip down again, like convection rain. But also mace and cloves and cinnamon and oranges; the scent of bread blooming into the room; sugar bubbling in pans over the flames, fruits doing the same.

But in the palace, I could not waste time in the kitchens, I could not bear to wait.

I took the route to the King's chambers that I had mapped on my first tour and played over in my head many times since. I walked in the middle of the corridors; I did not touch the walls or stop to look at paintings as I normally would.

I opened the King's door as if I had done it a thousand times, as if it were my own, and entered, like thread through the eye of a needle.

It was instant, the feeling: a whole world.

II

II

BETWEEN SHIFTS ATTENDING TO A DYING KING

The young Attendant to the King inspects the small pie – solid and pale, quite like a stone – and disappears half in one bite. He hasn't eaten since yesterday evening and the sun has been up for hours, concealed though it is behind a veil of cloud. Cloud the colour of slate. He picks up the leg of chicken and bites – when he pulls it away some of the roasted skin peels off and hangs from his mouth. The young Attendant chews this for a long time, the skin jiggling up and down and he unaware.

He is thinking about the slow and meandering journey to this death – how the King's breathing has changed over recent days, his head now moving up and down as if manipulated by string. He gasps for air, but there is no sound – also much like a puppet. The young Attendant finds this stage of breathing disturbing and hopes it will have passed by the time his next shift begins. He wonders whether the other attendants who have put in their share of witness also carry it into their dreams.

~

The King is young, married three summers ago. The young Attendant is perhaps only a year or two his junior, though he has never really thought of it before. He remembers clearly, amid the haze of his training – memorising names and preferences and timings and routes through the court and dislikes, learning when to speak and when not, who to look at and speak to and who to treat as a deity you may sense but cannot see, what had brought people favour and what had lost them their heads – being in attendance on the King's wedding night. The heat. The air almost wet. There is air that surrounds you and air you must move through, as if wading in a stream. How he stood outside the bed chamber with a silver bowl of water and rose petals, for hand washing. The muscles of his forearms howling with the ache of it. The petals very pale pink and fresh from the flower. *Be as if a statue*, was his order. When the noises began, he – and the other less experienced attendants – made alarmed eye contact, then smiled; some giggled and were shushed. They all looked down at the ground, burning. Hoping not to find themselves excited. Their elders, used to this ritual, carried on about their business, doing whatever it was they did. Moving things. Preparing towels or fruit, clearing their throats, pretending to write. The young Attendant would be lying if he said that those sounds hadn't floated into his imagination every now and then, when required.

The Queen had been younger than the King, only slightly. Shipped over from another court, another country – ensconced in fine blankets and furs on a boat, a fragile present in a very large box.

Arriving green from travel. Shocked silent by a brutal winter, she turned in on herself. A mouse preparing to hibernate, to lose half its body weight. And the darkness, she felt it loomed over her, sat at the end of her bed, crept up her back each time she was undressed. This she confessed to one of her ladies, fearing herself mad. But a Queen has no secrets, and so the King was told.

Who had contrived of this plan, to have such a delicate woman delivered here, in this season, when the air is colder than the grave? The King demanded to know. He demanded to know and he demanded that her happiness be secured. She was delivered fools and singers and musicians, books and wine, ladies to converse with, and fine, fine pastries. She nibbled and smiled weakly and made barely a sound.

The wedding was months in the devising, allowing time for elaborate plans and, crucially, for objections, which did not come. The future Queen must look favourably on her King, the court reasoned, for her to commit to a life in a climate so injurious to her. So, the wedding was planned, then delayed when the frost didn't lift. The ground, impenetrable, could not be dug for the planting of tender leaves and herbs. The over-winter potatoes and roots – essential for placating the commoners during the celebrations – were stunted by the severity of the cold. They needed time for a final flush into full growth.

The young Attendant saw more of the Queen-to-be when spring came, and she was brighter as she walked the gardens with her ladies. She lifted her face to whatever the sun could offer. She touched the flowers, she smelled everything. By the time the wedding came, the tulips were bare green stems, their petals fallen away to reveal their neat, angular necks, and the roses were opening their mouths.

So it was that the pale pink petals in a bowl of water in the young Attendant's burning arms on the wedding night, when it finally arrived, were a quite beautiful lesson in affection, and the ways in which it is communicated. The secret ways we may speak.

~

The Queen is dead two years already.

The young Attendant places a chunk of cheese onto a slice of ham and folds the ham around it like a parcel. He picks it up and takes a bite.

Sometimes he would open the King's chamber door for the Queen – delivered by candlelight, top to toe in white lace – and she would always smile her thanks to him.

After the Queen died the King had, for a while, barely eaten. He paid no more attention to the laden platters on his table than he did to the portraits of prospective new wives. One evening, at another silent dinner, the young Attendant had placed a cut of beef on the King's empty plate without being asked. Just sliced it and carried it to him. He had been, he tried to explain later, compelled. The King picked it up and ate it in one mouthful, not seeming to register what it was he conveyed into his mouth, while staring into a vague space ahead of him, presumably into his past. The young

Attendant had been immediately chastised for this act, pulled out of the room by his arm. *No one feeds the King besides the King, unless he expressly requests it. The King is not a baby.*

The young Attendant breathes in deeply. Holds it. Exhales at length. The chicken is trimmed with small potatoes which guard the perimeter of the plate – they have been placed in descending order by size. Such are the special details of the King's platters, which he now cannot eat, which get passed out to the attendants if the person on shift in the kitchen that day recognises hunger.

~

Last night the young Attendant tried to lie with his wife and couldn't do it. With every part of her body that was revealed, he saw also the King's, shining with sweat, twisting, floppy, cut open, dotted with leeches. He closed his eyes, really closed them, and smelled the bedroom of the King, stale and hot. He pushed into his wife and her moan was the sound of the King as he was roused for water. He pushed in again and heard the murmur of the physician conferring with his assistant as they poured out another hopeless tincture. His wife stilled him, placed a hand to his cheek. He looked down at her and saw the dead Queen, laid out in the chapel, her stomach still a small mound from the recent pregnancy. He had to stop. He could taste death in his mouth.

~

He is still holding the cheese and ham in his hand. He picks up a cup and drinks the contents.

MAY WE FEED THE DYING KING

Every day the same lady-in-waiting is sent up from the kitchens to ask the same question. More accurately, the essence of the question being asked is the same, but she varies her choice of words.

She knocks on the door, which is engraved and shining like the seed of a horse chestnut.

Day after day. Fist, knuckles, two raps.

The young Attendant to the King opens the door, steps into the hallway and closes the door gently. The room behind him – what she sees in the brief slice before the view is blocked – is dim, still, stale. There is a desperate look in his eyes – he seems to welcome this brief escape. He blinks slowly, he exhales.

She waits, then she speaks:

After one full day of his confinement: *Would his Majesty like anything to eat?*

The next morning: *May we prepare anything for his Majesty today?*

Slightly later on the third day, she fiddles an ulcer at the tip of her tongue with her front teeth: *We have very good thin salted mutton – perhaps his Majesty would care for some?*

On a day of howling wind – the trees being stripped: *And today, will it please the King to eat?*

After five days of not eating: *Does the King want for any refreshment? Perhaps a bone broth?*

Waking to discover a crow has flown into a window and lies splayed in the courtyard, unsettling the ladies: *The cook wonders whether we could tempt the King with a fruit jelly?*

It is a charade, both the question and the reply, which comes variously:

After one full day of his confinement: *His Majesty may well take a light supper.*

The next morning: *Perhaps a small bowl of stew would be wise. The aroma will surely tempt him.*

Slightly later on the third day, he scrapes down a strip of skin at his thumbnail with his forefinger: *I dare say when he next wakes he would relish a bite.*

On the day of howling wind – the sky spinning with leaves: *Today, yes, we are sure he will partake of something.*

After five days of not eating: *Why not a plate of stewed fruits, cut up small.*

Waking to word that a woman in the nearby village has foreseen the King's death and is preaching the ruin of the court: *The King has great love for a fruit jelly – we will try him with a morsel.*

It is a charade. It must play out. But it is a humiliating endeavour to ask a stupid question over and over to the same person, day after day. The young Attendant must also feel it.

Very well. Whatever his answer, she replies, *Very well.* Her head dips, she turns and sets off down the corridor and into the kitchens, to the anticipatory face of the master cook and his helpers.

They say to make his Majesty a morsel of something utterly delicious.

They say to make his Majesty something tempting.

They say to make his Majesty something plain.

They say to make his Majesty something soft and easy to chew.

They say to make his Majesty a broth, thick with marrow.

~

In the early days of the King's maladies, the ladies retrieving the plates would note the amount consumed. A few bites, a slice, a cause for celebration. These past days the plates have diminished by nothing, and when something appears reduced it is surely the work of the King's taster, or of a holy man who can no longer ignore the groans of his stomach after ten hours at the King's bedside. The plates are distributed among the staff in the kitchens and cellars, sent up to the attendants who are weary from their watch if there is enough to spare.

~

The lady-in-waiting who must ask after the King's appetite, hands behind her back and her head slightly bowed, was part of the royal household when there was a Queen. For a while after her death, the Queen's former ladies hovered about the apartments, mourning, putting things in order, making themselves useful but not too visible. Many hours were dedicated to the removal of blood from the quilts, bolsters and the bed itself. Then, nothing more to be done. Nothing but close the doors to the chambers and hope that time might cleanse the rooms of their grisly memories.

When it became clear that no replacement Queen was forthcoming, those of noble birth were directed back to their homes in the country and the rest were put to work elsewhere at court. The lady-in-waiting had been noted for her discretion and diligence – she was permitted to remain in service at the palace, tending to the lesser nobility.

RESURRECTION

The dying is really dragging on. No one can believe it.

Though no one wishes the King gone – beloved as he is, and he truly is – the young Attendant is sensing a tensing up within the court. A collective tetchiness. Similar to when a wasp, repeatedly swatted away, once again hovers at your food.

People can bear shock, and tragedy, and all manner of scandal, but this nothingness drives them mad. This enforced inaction. The sycophants may not fawn, the entertainers are idle, fiddling with their props. The stableboys lean against their doors and brush their horses perfect, the dubious men of business have nowhere to take their newly hatched schemes, the plotters can only speculate – which they hate – and the would-be-traitors are suspended as though flies in jelly. Which way to turn? Only the physicians and the holy men have anything to tend to, and there is a limit to the repertoire of both when the message does not change for weeks: the King must live; Almighty One, let the King live.

~

At a point the King even seemed better, looking less like wax, and nodded when someone asked if he was hungry, though he didn't eat. The young Attendant heard one of the holy men suggest it might be a miracle, but with an uplift in tone at the end, as if he were asking a question. And a stupid one. He would like nothing more than a miracle – anything that ends his constant state of queasiness – but even he half-smiles at the ridiculousness of the remark.

The King had no more than raised his head before a fellow attendant – bored, inexperienced, possessed by the prospect of delivering the news – escaped the room and bolted to the chamber where one hundred or so people were convened. They had been waiting in this room for many days, sure of imminent news and needing to be the first to hear it. The smell in that room was bad and growing worse. The people were tiring and regretting their initial zeal. *We couldn't have known*, they consoled themselves, *that the King's ailing would prove so . . . indeterminate.* But to leave now is unthinkable.

And so this attendant had his moment of glory – all eyes fixed on his face in wonder, people clutching their chests, gasping, cheering when he finished delivering his one idiotic line . . .

THE KING IS WELL!

They wanted to know more, pulling on his sleeves to get details. He was the fountain and they were many thirsty mouths. He would never feel more important again.

A senior attendant appeared behind him, pulled him backwards by the collar, spitting into his ear to keep his godforsaken mouth shut, calling him a fool. Jubilant shouts and claps followed them down the hall from the waiting room. This sound lodged itself in his dreams, and he often woke burning with the humiliation of it.

THE LIGHT

A morning of bright, cold sunshine. Today is the day, the physicians are sure.

The King's breathing is barely audible. They have been able to open the curtains now that the light doesn't seem to bother him.

He is elsewhere. They are at the precipice. Relief is coming.

THE CHEF HAS PREPARED A POTAGE

Again, she ascends the stairs from the kitchens – her ankles ache towards the top – with the question forming in her mouth.

How long can a person survive without food? It seems they are finding out.

The hallway to the King's quarters is windowless. There are paintings staring her down. Serious people in very fine clothes. Laced wrists, pearls at their lobes, eyes like glass. She wouldn't trust a single one of them.

The sconces on either side of the King's door depict fish with exaggerated mouths twisted into rolling gold waves. Large portraits flank the doorframe. To the left a child of around eight, with a cold, clenched face, one hand resting on a globe, the other on his thigh, in a fist. A small gilded sword hanging from his belt. On the wall behind him, a convoy of men on horses chopping down uprising peasants. A banner across the top reads ALL POWER TO THE KING. The eldest of the three brothers, dead so long now.

To the right, the King himself. Dying though he may be, he remains so. In his portrait he is relaxed but assured. The curls at his temples almost translucent. One hand resting on the holy book and the other on the head of a small marmot, which appears to smile. Sleeves of gold lace, an outrageously prominent codpiece. Stained glass in the background which throws exquisite, almost indiscernible fractals of light on the shoulder of his jacket. GOD PROTECT OUR PROTECTOR is written in small script at the bottom.

She raises a hand to knock. Stops. The room beyond the door is absolutely silent.

~

The young Attendant is in the room, in a far corner, when it happens.

He had expected a distinct moment, something clear, when the end came. Instead, one of the seated holy men stood, leaned over the King and placed an ear to his mouth. He gestured to the Senior Attendant to do the same. The Senior Attendant did so, then frowned, stood up fully, and lowered his head again, cupping his hand to his ear. He beckoned the King's Physician, seated at a desk beside his tinctures, scalpels and powders. The King's Physician rose, winced, placed a hand to his lower back, and approached the bed. He hovered a hand over the King's mouth and waited. He nodded and backed away. The same holy man placed one of the King's arms, then the other, across his chest, began his muttering.

73

The young Attendant cannot believe that death can occur so silently – just enter the room and leave again without so much as disturbing the curtains.

~

The lady-in-waiting remains by the door, lowers her hand. Something is altered. Altered as when you walk from an open field into the edge of a forest and the air becomes heavy.

She glances over her shoulder. How to proceed?

The door opens, very quickly. The young Attendant walks past her, disturbing the air with his speed. *No thank you*, he says.

~

The young Attendant returns to his room at a pace, takes off his hat and throws it on the table. He sits down and runs his hands through his hair, rests his forehead on his hands, elbows on the table, and cries.

At one point he works himself up to the point of inhaling very loudly, looks around the room as if for a vessel to be sick in, but calms down and takes a sip from his cup.

His wife isn't here to see him and he is glad of it. But also not.

~

He interrogates his memories, recalls the faces of the other men in the King's room. They barely changed.

The King is alive: their faces.

The King is dead: their faces still.

Not a flicker.

He thinks that there must be something very wrong either with him, or with other people.

THE KING IS DEAD,
LONG LIVE MY KING

The new King, the third in line, he is just as much chosen as the first and second. Everyone says.

Everyone says and the new King has heard little else in the days since his brother died. God's will, God's will, God in his unknowable wisdom, God who moves like water above, below and through us. The court is attempting an incredible self-deception. It is what it does best.

He wants to force someone to look him, unblinking, in the eye and listen to him say, *I know this is absurd, tell everyone that I know.* This is only possible with his wife, who must now become Queen at his side – she counsels letting the news settle on him, *like a petal on the surface of a pond.*

~

In his new rooms, in his new clothes, the new King sits at a table. A pile of documents awaiting his dead brother's signature. Manuscripts. An inkpot that wants filling, the smudge of his dead brother's finger on its silver plate. Two candles in fine copper sticks, engraved with constellations, as is the latest fashion. The light strange through the unfamiliar windows, the material of his collar bothering the skin of his neck.

He anticipated none of this. How is that possible? He is furious with himself.

~

His eldest brother he remembers so little of. On the throne a year, gone overnight. Still and blue-lipped as the sun rose. Secret relief for all those who knew his character, anticipated what he might become. His violence even then, as such a young boy – drawing the blood of nannies and playmates, whipping the horse too hard, enjoying that. His exasperated Regent discouraged the brutality. He had not expected this of a child. So many years have passed now. When people speak of the dead boy who sat on the throne, the little tyrant, the King often finds that he had forgotten there were ever three of them.

The second brother, on becoming King, allowed himself to be guided by his Regents and counselled by advisors; he learnt all he could for when he came of age. Without obsequiousness, made himself adored. By the time his rule began, he was charming, wise, could placate and cajole even the most outraged or disillusioned ally visiting court. As a man, he looked at any person in the palace – eligible or not – as if he might eat them whole. As if he might lick them all over and strip the meat from their bones. Few resisted. Why would they? A steady stream made their way towards his rooms, carrying wine and fruit and bowls of water, like ants with snippets of leaves. He was attentive in all ways. He remembered faces, occupations, the names of husbands and wives, children, their ages and particular gifts, the worrying dip in the timber of a house letting the rain in, the threat of its collapse. *How is the roof bearing up? I had no idea. Allow me to send someone.*

The new King recalls once, at an important dinner whose purpose eludes him now – and probably did even at the time – looking across at this brother and thinking, *He soaks everything up*. He felt himself a rock, absorbing nothing, reshaped over time by the will of the water. His brother was the meadow.

The coronation had been talked about for months after. A riot of colour and entertainment and feasting and his brother a beacon in the middle of it all. Not a single tremor, not a bead of sweat.

It was a golden era, they were living in it and felt it on their faces as sure as the warmth of the sun.

~

Some years of contentment and relative peace, the court famed for its hospitality, then the King's brother had grown tired. Perhaps slightly more than a person would expect of someone his age, and so buoyed by love for his wife, even accounting for the demands of the role. Suddenly, he appeared drained and ashen. He was sleeping more than usual, and clearly experiencing discomfort at the dinner table: he shifted in his seat, ate small mouthfuls of food, and made weak attempts at cheerful conversation. Began drifting during strategic conversations – his eyes quite empty. Once, in the night, he fell from bed – rigid then slack – and came round with no idea of his name or whereabouts.

The decline was quick but the death had been slow. Slow and meandering. Gruesome, quite honestly. He had visited his dying brother infrequently, hating all of it and sensing himself the person no one in the room dared acknowledge. The dreaded alternative. But when he did muster the fortitude, or was told that his brother had asked for him, he felt that the King's body was being *inflicted upon*. It was being *done to*. So much cutting and bleeding and sweating, and placing objects in soft flesh that was so clearly beyond redemption.

One night he dreamt that they cut his brother's arm open to bleed him and the meat of him was tinged green.

~

If he is completely truthful, he doesn't think he really knew his brother would die until someone stated it as a matter of fact. *When you are King*, they had said to him, forgetting themselves. Then clamped a hand to their blasphemous mouth.

~

What was he then, the third brother? How would anyone describe him? As a child, he had been the one permitted to roam the grounds, take lessons with a friend, pet the sheep in the fields. He was allowed to become odd. Naturally he was schooled in many subjects, became proficient in riding, knew the holy texts, and understood the customs and expectations that dictated a life such as his. But he was never in the direct line of sight; he was always two seats left of centre.

He has often wondered whether his entire person has been shaped by what he was – and wasn't – in relation to his brothers. He was not the wood or the worm, but the hole that spoke of its presence. Not the person or the chair, but the indent left behind on the seat.

~

The elders are trying, in their letters abroad, to conjure a sense of the man:

The new King? God save him. Temperate? Very. On his way to being wise, surely. For an almost young man.

He will produce heirs quickly, we have no doubt. The Queen, while also not as young as we might hope, is healthy and strong.

He has a noble look in his eyes and never speaks without first thinking carefully.

He is yielding, mouldable, yet only as a plant which rots at the surface, preparing to come back next season, not changed but stronger than before.

Perhaps, they wondered, this is a gift from God: a King who can be remade in a winter.

~

So it was, on a summer morning two decades ago, as he sat at his lessons drawing an elaborate mythical creature in the margins of his parchment, *The King is dead, Long live the King*. Then, on an afternoon in late winter only days ago, as he wrote a letter to a childhood friend, *The King is dead, Long live the King*.

The duty placed on him like a boulder on the chest of a sleeping man.

GLIMPSES

Someone looking in through the window to the new King's quarters would see the door opening, as the King enters.

He turns to his men and holds up a hand in front of his chest, his palm facing them.

His mouth forms a request to be left alone for a moment to pray. He accompanies this request by raising the hand upwards, pointing to the sky.

The door closes.

His face is that of a person who is coming to understand that they have relinquished all control of their life, and yet can make any demand they like. It is the face of one who has just woken from a nightmare.

He removes his cloak – oxblood silk embroidered with gold thread – and lays it on the bed. He looks at the cloak in a manner that could be interpreted in three ways:

1) He cannot believe it belongs to him

2) He wishes to burn it

3) He is not looking at the cloak at all

The new King sits at his unfamiliar desk in a room that until a few short days ago belonged to his brother. The new King sits at an unfamiliar desk and lowers his face into his hands.

WE CANNOT KNOW GOD TRULY,
BUT WE WILL TRY

This new King moves through the first days of his rule in wild turns – he is stunned, horrified, disbelieving, resigned, aghast, furious.

There has been one certainty at the centre of his life: that he would never be King. Who has stolen this from him? In his solitary questioning he begs to know.

~

He is shunted from place to place. He is advised, guided, instructed. He is seated. He is bidden to stand up again and *please follow me, my Lord*. He puts something down, it is picked up for him. He is summoned by someone, by many people – he has no choice but to go.

There are knocks at the door, papers to sign, meetings to attend. He must be briefed on this matter, on another matter, *it is pressing, it is imperative*.

He barely sleeps. He barely sees his wife.

He is a moth and the candle is in constant motion.

~

His council put his oddness – what else to call it? – down to the shock of grief, the great jolt into this strange life. The new King often appears on the verge of tears. He seems lost. Not even the merest glimmer in his eyes that betrays a hunger for power, that he has finally got what he dared before only dream of.

He has lost two brothers, they say, *this situation was foreseen by no one besides God – God who can move so strangely, God in his unknowability. He will settle.*

THE QUEEN

The new King at least has a wife, which is some consolation, so the ladies of the former Queen's household are dredged up from their various dark corners, recalled from boredom in their country houses. They flock like chickens to scattered feed.

The new Queen's rooms are turned over from top to bottom – rugs smacked in the courtyard, floors scrubbed, treated with linseed oil and varnished, curtains and drapes washed and dried. She is consulted as to her preferences, her tastes, her demands. She insists that she is very comfortable where she is.

Comfortable is not good enough.

~

The new Queen is spirited, neat – a totally contained person. Women like her immediately, men think her unfoolish. Her mother had been ambitious in her plans for her daughter's life – perhaps even ambitious enough to secure her a King – but she had

86

said, *no, a little freedom, I beg you.* So, a brother was settled upon – a brother who would certainly never rise so high.

She has been in love with another man at court since around two years into her marriage to the now-King. He is Assistant to the Royal Physician. He was called one day to attend to her persistent head pain when his superior was otherwise engaged, and as he rubbed oil expertly into her temples she felt her body respond as if his hands were reaching inside her.

The King also likes him very much. The incumbent physician hobbles about the room seeming to forget where he is and what is expected of him – reaching for the bloodletting knife with a regularity that at best belies an inability to keep up with the developments in his profession, and at worst, well . . . He also carries an air of doom, which is unfortunate. But his assistant, the Queen's lover, is reassuring, unshakeable, able to distract a patient with his kindness. He handles a twisted or mutilated or gangrenous limb as if it is a side of ham at the butcher's that he is willing to pay handsomely for. All flesh has value and is treated accordingly.

Prior to the great change in their situation, the now-Queen and her lover were granted some rooms at court – a bedroom, a washroom and a little lounge for playing cards and taking meals. There they were able to live together well, and privately. It was the only thing the now-King ever asked of his dead brother, who granted it on the condition that they would be afforded no household. The gossip would have been salacious and constant. He did not want his brother to be spoken of as a fool in the dim of the court's many hidden chambers.

WHAT OF THE SAUCEPAN

The kitchens set about understanding their new Lord's palate.

The former King favoured fish, sweet puddings and pastries. He took great pleasure in a sudden ring of flavour, as afforded by a pickled vegetable or a curd of citrus.

This King seems to eat out of necessity rather than pleasure. He calls for nothing specific, demands no delicacies, sends nothing back in disgust, throws nothing across the room at his staff, does not summon the cooks to his room and force them to eat what they have prepared, to tell him to his face if they think what they have presented is fit for a King.

There is time yet for him to understand quite how much is at his disposal. For him to learn what people will tolerate.

DEFLATE

Someone looking in through the new King's window – the rectangular window on the garden side, which frames a conifer – would see the King look up from his papers as the door opens.

The Queen enters. Her shoulders drop when she sees him, as if, until that moment, her body had been enduring the discomfort of remaining totally upright, rigid with air. She moves towards him at a pace and holds his face in her hands. She looks back at the door to make sure they are alone, before turning back to him. She begins to speak; the movements of her mouth are small. The new King grips the material at her waist, leans his face forward into the teal and silver embroidery of her stomach. Her hands move to the back of his neck. No more than a few breaths pass – she places her fingers under his chin and lifts his face to hers. She speaks again, and the King's head remains raised. The Queen nods slowly and smiles – as when a parent encourages a small child. The King shakes his head almost imperceptibly.

Their heads whip in the direction of the door. A knock. Without being beckoned, someone is entering.

HOW TO CARE ABOUT POWER

Almost two weeks have passed since the death of the last King, since the new one was so abruptly summoned, required to hand over his life.

The court continues to mourn, so the people mourn still. The new King keeps his head bowed and lurks in the shadows of this great collective grief. He will have to emerge soon – surely – presenting himself to the people in his mourning clothes. It will be expected that he tower above them on a huge black stallion.

~

The new King is horrified by the regularity with which he is expected to sign away life. One person, a small group, an entire fleet – numbers don't seem to matter. He is given little information, details are not necessary. All it would take is his word, a nod, a flick of the wrist. He had no idea that this had been required of his brother, who floated through the court's luminous rooms as if he had never inflicted harm on even the merest creature.

~

The King has a sense that he will need to develop a stomach for bloodshed if he is to survive – he might take his numbness and put it to good use.

He is urged: how else will the country hold its power if its King does not become inured to the wet thud of a subject on the cobblestones? Surely, if nothing else, the King is the country's greatest murderer – faceless and clean of hand.

An opportunity comes. The Queen suggests it and he has no better idea. He is rudderless, grateful to have a task set for him. He remembers some years ago a friend who had lost his wife and child in the same year saying that in his head he chose to live in a time before their passing. That he resented being pulled into the present. But the present for the King is everywhere – it is a banshee wailing in his ear.

He wants to get out of these rooms, away from these eyes and the perfume in which he is constantly doused.

A father and son imprisoned after trial for treason against his brother – what, five years ago? – and left to grow foetid in a cell. They were once previously brought to the block to get the job done. Word reached them and the amassed crowd after more than an hour that the executioner was languishing with fever, would likely die, and certainly could not come to despatch them that day. His late brother's signature is now not valid.

One day, an advisor remembers that these men exist, comes across the old paperwork, says that places are running low in the gaol and that they could do with freeing up some space. They have all manner of criminals and vagrants stuffed into the dungeon below the main tower, and among them a couple of noblemen who should at least be afforded a room with a desk, a chamber pot and a hard plank on which to lay their heads. The advisor brings it to the King at council – hands over the decree for a signature. The King queries whether the crime, committed many years ago and against a person no longer living, remains therefore a crime. He is assured that the sentence on treason does not expire – contempt for the crown is a lifelong affliction. A week passes, two. Their names have floated back and forth across the council chamber, the King has ignored the decree or obscured the papers beneath others one too many times, enough times to make people talk. But of what? Weakness? Sympathy? *Master, a King who cannot send a message will soon have no audience to hear it.*

~

The insistence of his advisors that he must do this is still haunting his ears; they hardly bothered to conceal their disgust.

He smooths the decree out on the table and with shaking hand dips the quill into the inkpot. He hesitates so long with it hovering above the paper that the ink drips where his signature should be. *You may sign anywhere, my Lord.*

They are sniffing him out for what he is.

The next day, rising early, not eating, he goes to see what the elegant curl of his ink can do.

~

Later that day, someone looking in through a crack in the door – were it by chance the day when the boy who is forgetful when it comes to door shutting is on shift at the entrance to the King's apartments – would see the King at his table with three advisors chatting happily around him, drinking his wine and eating his food. The King responds only when spoken to. He looks pale and grim, almost determined, his jaw tight. The advisors are happy with the King's display. *You cheered loudly, my lord, when the axe came down. That was well done. The people noticed that.*

The advisors begin to joke about the looks on the faces of the now deceased. *One of them pissed himself, did you see?* The King looks around the room as if there might be someone in the shadows who can save him.

Not the cleanest job I've seen. The advisor who says this picks up a small cleaving knife and brings it down repeatedly on the chicken leg, exposing the white flesh under the roasted skin and pulping it. One of the other advisors laughs so hard he becomes red and can't swallow his wine, shaking a hand out in front of him to beg his friend to stop.

~

Finally, he is being undressed for bed. The light shines through his shirt when he lifts his arms to a T – the outline of his body hard and defined as a shadow.

~

The men had been dirty and thin, seeming long since to have abandoned any notion of making themselves decent for a public death. The necks and cuffs of their shirts were ringed with a yellow like dark urine.

Will they need to be brought forth and held down, the King had wondered, or else will they rush forward to get it done, throw themselves down on the block? What would he do? He asked the Queen at dinner the night before if she had ever seen a life taken in front of her. She had attended a beheading as a child and closed her eyes even before the axe had been raised. She didn't open them again until she was being led away by the hand. *But you*, she said, *you must keep your eyes open. You must appear to revel in it, if you can.*

The winter sun had been low, and the men dithered side by side, squinting, not sure where to step or who should go first. They looked about vaguely as if seeking direction. The son recognised someone in the crowd, a young man of a similar age to him, and froze briefly. The young man in the crowd tried to push his way to the front but was eaten up by the mass of bodies ahead of him. The crowd grew impatient. Someone threw something – a chunk of bread? A potato? – at the son who, jolted from his indecision, stepped forward, said something inaudible to the crowd and dutifully knelt at the block. Then, a pause, and the father stepped forward, said something the King couldn't make out over the babble – perhaps wishing to go first as a matter of honour? Perhaps overwhelmed by the imminent fact of his son's death, and of his having to witness it and exist in the world without him, even briefly. But it came too late, and instead the son's head twisted slightly at his father's call as the axe came down, awkwardly, on the diagonal, clipping the bottom of the ear, and not quite making it through the whole neck. The axe was pulled up, out from the wound, as if stuck in the trunk of a felled tree. Then it was swung down again. The father, shaking his head left then right, almost comically, like a man on stage, a gesture too big for the scene. He was then grabbed by the collar, pulled forward, to the ground, despatched in an instant. A roar of approval from the crowd; a sound escaping from the King's mouth, quite without intention.

The person who had thrown the pale lump at the son had chewed their way through all this without stopping. The King marvelled at the constitution of their stomach.

~

The King believes he will think of this decision for the rest of his days. A few bites into a meal, a detail will come to him – the executioner's spit, a thick globule on the platform, wobbling, or the filthy feet of the father standing in the warm blood of his son. A while into pleasuring himself before he sleeps, even then, the glistening pink of just-exposed flesh will appear. It lurks in his mind like the shadow of a fish, always just below the surface.

That night, he lies awake thinking not of the two men he has killed that day, but of the young man in the crowd, the glimpse of his desperation. How he has forever altered the course of his life.

TO BE DIRTY

The King is alone, praying in his chambers.

There are two men positioned on the other side of the door, shuffling. Occasionally one of them clears his throat, lifts his staff and resets it against the floor.

The King's household think him very pious – so far, it is the only thing they can honestly say about him in the affirmative, so they say it often and loudly. They are testing this out as his defining identity, in lieu of any better alternative.

The King prays often, in public. He knows what a praying person looks like and how they should behave. It is an easy part to play. He closes his eyes and mutters words he has known by heart his whole life. He strongly suspects that no one is listening to him.

The King requests time alone in his chapel to commune with God. The quiet then is absolute, as if his entire head has been set in a room-sized jelly, and no one may force him out. He also insists on being left alone to pray in his rooms, when there is a break in the demands on his time. He uses this time to touch things that would otherwise be forbidden.

He sweeps the ash from the fireplaces. He starts carefully, cursing quietly when he gets a speck or smudge on his cuff, then he begins to worry less. What is more dirt on top of dirt? No one will dare to question him about the state of his clothes or of his person. Now there is black grit behind each of his fingernails. He spits on his hands before he tries to wipe them clean. Sometimes he puts a finger inside his nostril to feel its interior.

His favourite thing, if one of his cats has jumped up and in through the window, is to wipe the crust from the corners of their eyes with his thumb. To feel their bellies for tiny scraps or seeds they have carried in from the garden. He places his nose next to their mouth and smells the stink of their breath.

Sometimes, when he is alone with his favourite cat and she jumps up to his lap, she butts her nose into his stomach, his neck. He cradles her as he has seen parents cradle their children. She is ash grey, with one white ear and white front paws, as if in bed socks. He imagines that in this world there exist only the two of them, and she relies on him and him alone, never flinching at a sudden noise or movement. She lets her head be easy and her tail drape over his sleeve. Her noises of contentment moving through his arm. It feels like pure joy.

He was caught in this position by one of his attendants – perhaps three years ago, before he was King. Now the rumour has new life, as if it happened only yesterday. Walking through the main rooms at court he is sure he feels the prickle of gossip in the air.

The King is so mad for want of a child he believes his cat to be one. Perhaps the Queen tries to nurse it.

CAN A MAN BE FLAYED
AND HIS HIDE WORN?

The court, the noble families, the Church, all the common people of the land – they are baby birds, mouths open and trembling for news of their new ruler.

His advisors are becoming increasingly agitated. *It is time your rule began, my Lord. You must show them something of your person.*

They coax him to hunt, to fell a boar for a feast, to sling it over his shoulder and enter the palace as if he were carrying no more than a cloak of silk. He refuses the kill but joins the hunts, at least to be seen to ride out of the palace gates with a pack of men and with bows on his back. The people seem to like that.

The motion of the horse soothes him, the hot breath escaping its nostrils, its ability to intuit what the King wants from it, although he doesn't truly know this himself.

But the uneasiness of life leaving the eyes of rabbits and deer, the chaos of feathers as pheasants plummet to the ground, their limp bodies swinging a nauseating rhythm as they are conveyed back to the palace: it settles on him like a chill that he cannot shake for hours.

~

One of the kinder advisors has suggested to the King that it might do him well to consider a project of his own – something notable that he will be remembered for. It would be a good focus for his mind. The King feels he would rather prefer to disappear without a trace than be remembered by anyone, but he resolves to put his mind to it when he is alone.

His brother, so recently dead the King still forgets it, favoured exploration. He had announced plans to commission a new fleet of ships which would travel further than any man has ventured, seeking out new lands with their fruits, vegetables and spices.

The King allows himself to wonder what his oldest brother might have planned, had he lived into adulthood. Perhaps an elaborate expansion of their territories – a bolstered land army, new weapons and innovative warfare. He could certainly have had the idea of controlling trade routes and limiting supplies to would-be enemies, starving them into surrender or else weakening them for the attack. He would have reasoned: why waste the bodies of strong men, and ammunition, when you can squeeze people from afar? In the council chamber, the King remembers, he had a map of the known world spread out on the table, miniature ships whittled from bone marking the land he wanted. Domination, an amusing game for a child. These musings serve as a helpful counter to what the King may do, if ever he does anything.

~

Alone at his table now, picking at a plate of sliced ham with pincered thumb and finger, the King is thinking about his dead brothers and his new project.

The weight of his unhappiness is so palpable it emanates from him like a smell.

Papers sit in a pile at the edge of the table – all requesting violence, a royal sanction for it. All unsigned.

~

The Chief Advisor – the one he has inherited from his brother – puts him on edge. This Chief Advisor is the son of his father's advisor, who was also advisor to the King before him. He regularly cracks the knuckles of his bony, agitated hands. The King wonders – is there not, surely there must be a way to stop this inheriting? It cannot be true that each of these men is born ready to advise. Surely they enter the world clueless as an egg dropped from a hen, much like all people, much like him?

His Chief Advisor emanates the energy of the clergy. Judgemental, always disappointed, easily cruel. Entitled, eerily calm in his requests, until he is not. Then he appears possessed. When he enters a room without warning the King feels the blood drain from him. It feels like rain falling through his entire body.

~

The cat meows at the King's feet, rubs its cheek across his shin, and his face breaks. He leans in, breaks off a piece of ham and lowers it to the cat's mouth.

IN BETWEEN SHIFTS
ATTENDING TO THE NEW KING

The young Attendant to the King still sees the ailing body of the now-dead King in the moment before awake turns to asleep. He thinks about the dead King's body, now in its sarcophagus, and ponders the stage of decay. How long has it been? Four weeks? He has nothing to go on, never having seen anything rot but apples and potatoes.

He wants to ask other people if this response is out of the ordinary. He wants to know the thoughts of others without exposing his own.

~

But there is a new King to think about now, in addition to the one who lies on his back in the crypt. The young Attendant watches this new King, who wears the face of a man dropped into the middle of the ocean without warning. Sometimes the King becomes aware of this and tries to adjust his features accordingly, but it remains there in his eyes:

Horror.

When he attends to the King during the early-morning shift, he delays as much as possible the moment when he must throw back the bed curtains and bid him a good morning. He knows this will end whatever peace sleep brings him.

MONITOR HIS PLATE

The cooks are doing everything they can. The master of the kitchen is exhausting his repertoire, pulling on his beard in desperation, churning out dish after dish. They all return untouched, or barely depleted. The King eats like a mouse. The undercooks, servers and cupbearers descend upon the voluminous leftovers. The nobility joke that at least their Lord is approved of by the servants – they have never before in their lives eaten like Kings.

~

There is a story told in the kitchens to warn hungry staff against eating food that was meant only for royal mouths: a hundred years ago, maybe two, a King was feasting at the sprawling, varnished sycamore table of the great hall. The feast was colossal, with golden platters lining the entire length of the table. At the end of the evening, the King noticed that a ring – an incredibly fine and valuable ring, with a diamond the size of a grape circled by the deepest sapphires – was missing from his finger. He recalled that this particular hand with this particular finger had probed inside the head of the roasted pigs, scooping out the cheeks, that it had plunged into a pie to find the penny, that it had handled all manner of sticky puddings and sweets, even down to the jelly set in the shape of a lion. The platters were searched thoroughly, as was the ground beneath the table and the seats, as were the corners behind the drapery. The fingers of the other guests were inspected. When the ring was not found the King's mind turned to the staff – not only those scurrying in and out carrying jugs and trays, but those in the bowels of court, those he could not see. Those not fit to emerge and look him in the eye. He ordered that all the staff were to be searched, stripped if necessary. If that were to prove fruitless, an advisor pondered – merely pondered – that perhaps the staff who ate the leftovers should be returned to the kitchen and questioned. That perhaps one of them may have eaten the ring by accident – or even not by accident at all, spotting their one chance at the perfect crime. The chance gleaming out at them, from the pig's head, like a star. The staff were questioned; they said they had eaten not one bite of the discarded feast. Not one of them, not one bite. The soldiers set about smelling the mouths of the staff, inspecting the crevices in their back teeth to see what might be lodged therein. Of course they had all eaten. Every one of them. This was reported to the King and, furious, he demanded them all slit from the chest to the pubis. *Show me their stomachs!* he had raged. And so he was shown.

~

The King enjoys fruit in its raw form. This is a source of great concern for the Royal Physician, who knows this to be a dangerous method of consumption. He recommends baking it into pies or preserving it in honey – much better for there to be some human intermediary between what nature offers us and our mouths.

~

The Queen advises the King to perform an appetite, at least when he is hosted by other people. People who take him away from his quarters, all making a case for something or other, scrabbling for favour like crazed dogs. She says that he must appear healthy, and as if his duties demand of him so much energy that he always needs filling up.

A King who doesn't want to eat surely barely lifts a finger? they may otherwise ponder. *How will he master a horse, and swipe men down in battle, if he cannot tear meat from a bone?*

The Queen says that in her country it is said that not feeding the King is worse than starving the people.

LOOP

Every day he wakes in his bed. If it is not dark, he observes the conifer through the window. Every day he wakes in his bed and he cannot believe what has happened to him. He listens for birds. The shape of the conifer is so pleasing. When he wakes he tries to remain still, tries not to alert the attendants in the room. Before long someone always checks, or notices a change in his breathing, or he must clear his throat and give himself away. They notice and they say *Good morrow, my Lord.* They announce to the room *The King is risen!*

Every day starts in this way, with a statement he is unable to refute. He feels a thud of panic – the quiet kind. Like a stone dropped in a pond, and the tremor that follows.

~

The King has, so far, refused the many suggestions, as well as the few insistences and the one demand, that he assemble men for battle. Not even to quash a small uprising in a backwards little village withholding its taxes. No, he will not despatch just a few armed men to check whether the disease among the animals they claim has left them starving is a fabrication. Not even to dig around in the church coffers to see what they're hiding, to bloody a few noses. He is informed that his brother did this without even blinking, that this is what is expected. He is told these things almost kindly, as if he is a child who simply does not understand. He is informed that if the troops are not put to action with regularity, they become weak, their muscles thin. *The men are bred for this, to assert their physical power over another – I leave you to imagine where that power is channelled when there is no enemy to absorb it. Better to keep them tight, limber and primed for battle – they enjoy these small forays into violence.*

With the passing days and weeks, the King's non-compliance starts to be read by half as defiance, by the other half as cowardice. The council do not like it.

One morning, the Chief Advisor becomes so frustrated at the King's refusal to do as he is bidden, at the total absence of zeal and hankering for bloodshed, at the *unshakeable tendency towards inaction which, frankly, is starting to feel like it needs to be shaken out,* that he spits a little on the King's sleeve. *Would you have us be an anvil, my Lord, bashed by everyone around us?*

The King feels the Chief Advisor wants to gut him and wear his skin as a costume. Just to make things happen. He does understand. When a person defines themselves by their power to influence, if that is all they know, and it is taken away from them – well, then they punch out into the dark.

CULTIVARS AND HYBRIDS

Sometimes the Queen stays the night in the King's bed.

They sit and eat together first – the King often picking at morsels, which he chews at length, trying to appreciate the flavour, the Queen taking larger bites and seeming to enjoy getting her fingers a little dirty. She has a small gap between her front teeth in which a stubborn herb will often lodge itself. The King gently taps his upper lip with his forefinger to let her know. Often, she picks up a whole chicken leg – the King is more inclined towards dividing a small pie up into neat little segments, like an orange. The Queen gives the King a hard look and he reaches out for another handful. She taps his foot with hers under the table as the plates are cleared and he looks up to the young Attendant, says *Please thank the cook for his efforts – they are appreciated. Tell him that the King ate well. If it pleases you, take whatever you would like.*

One evening of frowning sky and rain, the King asks the Queen how is the Assistant to the Royal Physician? Are they content together, has her ascent to Queen made things burdensome for them? She replies that they are – they are managing it well. She asks whether the King has had a change of heart about the arrangement, whether it is upsetting to him to be called cuck by the court.

The King thinks. The King says he wishes for nothing but her happiness, and he knows only too well how this change in their circumstances has diminished it, despite what she says. He is so sorry for it. He confesses his envy, however, for the way her lover is allowed to live. His usefulness, his ease, his freedom to get dirty, to lay his hands on whatever he wants. The King sees a cloth he likes, reaches for it to test between his fingers, perhaps to smell, and it is whipped into the air and presented to him. The King sees an apple he would like to pick and someone is called for to free it from the branch, after which it is washed, polished. He passes a geranium shrub in the garden, comments that he wishes to select a flower for the Queen, knowing how she loves the smell. He wants to pause, assess the shrub, snip his chosen stems and keep walking, discussing whatever godforsaken matter of war is at hand with green between his fingers. This is not possible. He is told it will be arranged, and later when the Queen returns to her quarters she will find a tiny vase of geranium flowers on the table, pink and anonymous.

He is unable to be dishonest about the facts as they are: that he wants her lover's life.

~

At a point in the evening, the Queen returns to her quarters to dress for bed. She is then escorted back to the King, decked neck

111

to floor in a heavy laced fabric, and delivered to him, framed in his door like a saint in a glass window. This was necessary even before he was King. His brother went so far as to call him to his quarters one day. *Everyone knows about the Queen and her man, but you must appear to be having her as well, at least when we have foreign ambassadors at court. You know well what people already say.*

So, she was prepared, wrapped up and presented to him once a week.

~

It is more important now than ever that this happens. The new King understands this. He understands everything, despite appearances. He and the Queen agree between them that she will divide her time between his chambers and her lover's more equally – that she'll place a few more coins on his side of the scale.

~

A person looking in through a very small crack in the large, dark, varnished door would see the King lift the Queen's veil. They would see him address his attendants, who then leave the room promptly. The door closes and the King and Queen lie down together, muttering in the dark. They speak themselves into sleep, telling stories of their childhood or the great change to their circumstances, and how they will be able to bear it.

They wake entwined, clothed, and this is how they stay until someone sees them and bids them good morning.

PUSSY

Rumour is that the King began to cry during council.

The story that seeps out from that central chamber, from the sloppy mouth of the junior record keeper, is that the King was being urged, and not for the first time, to consider an offer of alliance from a nearby country – poorer, but with a larger army, famed for its wildness in battle. The court is sure that many of the stories they have heard about their conduct on the battlefield can't possibly be true – they are beyond the imagination. The Chief Advisor, to emphasise the point, kept extending his arm in front of him and saying things like, *They are offering a hand of friendship.* Jutting it out like a rod and gripping his wrist with his other hand. *They are reaching out to us and we need simply reach back.*

Briefly, the King got stuck into this rhetoric, seeming to quite enjoy the theatre of it, countering with, *When the arm is extended, is that not when the wrist is exposed?* – running a finger across the skin of it, the raised veins – *One hand in the grip of another is surely no different to a hand tied behind the back?*

Some of the other advisors had even found themselves murmuring in agreement. *The King makes a point.*

The Chief Advisor – briefly sporting – began to lose patience, feeling himself mocked. He grew louder, more insistent, urged the King once more and then again to consider this offer, to consider what it would do for their defences, their borders, their reputation.

Men are not cheap, my lord, and they are offering them to us.

In return for what? the King asked.

The Chief Advisor gestured as if throwing away a handful of air.

A share of whatever land or peoples we win together. The details would need to be arranged. The specifics are not your concern, my Lord.

The story goes that the King then made to leave the room and was blocked by the Chief Advisor, who told him – his mouth almost touching the King's nose – that his father would be disgusted with him, that his brothers would be laughing at him, if they could see the way he is behaving: *like a horse bolting from the hunt.*

The King turned to face the wall, made a small noise like a whimper and muttered something which one person heard as *Help*, another as *You are right*. The advisor to the King's left swears he said, *Stop it*; the Chief Advisor himself heard, *You will regret this.*

~

It is a rumour that many people actually choose not to share, finding the words so shameful to speak aloud. But they will listen when someone chooses to speak on it – everyone is comfortable with that.

~

A person who happened to be present that morning, sitting silently on the bed like a spirit, would have seen that a host of men had visited the King's room to discuss plans for the coronation. The King was barely up and washed when they descended, laying silks over his shoulder, measuring his head, making suggestions for what fine jewels the King might want about his neck and on his fingers – may they be so bold as to suggest sapphires so as to call to mind the sea, and assurances of exploration of unknown shores, trade deals, an army that will conquer foreign lands and all the oceans between them. And perhaps rubies and garnets for the Queen, clustered into formations that resemble pomegranates, all beset with freshwater pearls and opals. *Fertility and purity, my Lord, fertility and purity.*

She would look like a bleeding mouth, was the King's reply.

They encouraged the King to practise his sitting and rising, imagining a significant weight upon his head, his hands preoccupied with the holding of a staff and an orb. *You will need to engage the strength in your torso, my lord. You will need to be sure you can keep your left hand raised, holding a significant weight, for quite some time, for at least the length of one blessing. Will that be possible, my*

Lord? We recommend a regular routine of practice. To lower your hand would be—

The King raised his eyes in anticipation of the end of the sentence, which did not come.

A BOX WITH A LID

The King is circled in on, like injured prey on a mountaintop.

He startles at a hand on the door, a tankard clattering to the flag-stones, a sudden cheer in a game of cards.

His unhappiness, it grows and grows, and nothing is happening.

~

Nothing is happening.

His council say this cannot continue – they say this with one voice, which he finds incredible. One speaks on behalf of them all and he wonders when they came to this agreement. Or else they hum a low note, or look into their laps as they raise a hand, *Aye*, in unison.

They say *My Lord there is much to be done.*

My Lord the country does not run itself.

My Lord a boat with no one at the stern will run itself into the rocks.

My Lord a fatherless country learns no discipline.

My Lord a body without a head bleeds out while the corpse still twitches.

There is much to be done but truly the King does not see what. Trade takes care of itself – by who knows or cares what machinations? – the harvest has been plentiful, sickness has yet to sweep through the court this season, and as far as he is concerned, the people may worship as they please. He just needs time to pass, he just needs to make it through some more days and then weeks and eventually, surely, he will find himself standing in a meadow, unafraid and not King.

His council, his devil advisors, gather like flies and land, and land, and land on his hands and leg and face and will not be batted away – they are a swarm on a pile of horseshit that lifts and returns, lifts and returns each time a carriage thunders by. They demand executions, the crushing of skirmishes, *perhaps a little more tax, perhaps a war somewhere exotic and not too close to home, too far for the gangrenous injured to return from and burden us with their wounds, too far for anyone at court to lose a foreign cousin, why not send out some explorers once again on a fine boat as your brother, rest his soul, had great plans to do, why not raise taxes ever so slightly on the farmers, it was after all a plentiful harvest, why not a feast to toast our King, why not a tournament of games, a bear fight, a cock fight, wrestling, theatre, magic, ladies dancing, jokers, fools, why not.*

The King must also approve all marriages among his court and frankly he finds it hard to care who weds who – it is a custom he has always found strange, that a King may approve or disallow who another person takes to bed, lives alongside, bears children with. A request comes from a Lord of somewhere who wishes to wed a cousin of the Queen. He signs. The Chief Advisor, snatching away the papers, remarks that it would seem the King has no more control over the Queen's cousin than he does over the Queen herself. Had the King not considered the tactical possibilities of using the Queen's female relatives – in the absence of any heirs – to build allegiances? Does he not understand how valuable noblewomen are – that they may be sent anywhere and people will pay handsomely for them? Of course he does not; of course he squanders them.

JEZEBEL

He says to the Queen when he is sure no one else is listening at the door, *I am not made for this.*

Her reply comes: *You cannot have been the only one.*

~

Sometimes the King feels he must sleep just to be alone.

He misses his old rooms: the smell of them, the view out onto the rose gardens, the small birds flitting in and out of the shrubbery. The freedom to walk, to browse the library, to sit and write a letter to someone he truly cares for about something that interests him. For that letter not to be read before it is sent. For that letter not to be discreetly thrown in the fire without his knowledge.

COMFORT

When the King's shock has settled, he finds that his other feelings come into focus.

Loneliness, like a terrible cave.

His companions from before he was King, select though they were, now bow to him, and won't turn their backs to leave a room. When he is able to receive their company in his chambers, they are stiff and uncomfortable, despite his assurances.

There are men who seek to attach themselves to power, and there are those who do not. For some, a King is the cure, and for others, he is the disease.

So, the King asks for his young Attendant. The gentle boy who assisted his brother so diligently in his final weeks. He sees something in his eyes and would like him in his company.

The young Attendant is summoned and instantly fears for something. A summoning is never good – setting yourself apart is never good. Not with a King. He is called for and he follows the bobbing head of his fellow attendant, whose neck in front of him is visible in a finger's width and then not in the tide of his collar. So much distance between them now, now that he is an attendant who has been summoned. He walks briskly and quietly, not making conversation, not even clearing his throat. He makes to ask what all this is about, if he knows anything, but thinks better of it.

Outside the door. The dark and shining door which he knows to be lighter than it looks. It is opened for him and he is obliged to step forward, into the gleaming open space. The King looks up. *Come,* he says. *Please sit.*

The King apologises for this intrusion into the young Attendant's day. He asks after the young Attendant's wife, if he has one, and after his general health. *You tended to my brother as he died,* the King says, with a directness that is reassuring. The young Attendant responds that he did, that it was his honour. *Visiting his bedside made me feel sick,* says the King. *Sick in a way I cannot forget. What do you think that says about a man?*

ENQUIRIES, MERELY

The coronation looms.

It is discussed daily. His staff speak of it with no enthusiasm, they who will bear the extra work. But there is also the feast, as well as the subsequent games, so . . .

The King's despair is wide and deep as a lake.

The setting of the sun in the late afternoon is at its most brutal this time of year – gone in a blink. Then, a deep darkness. The King looks to the window beside the bed, through which he is used to seeing the outline of a great conifer. Not tonight. Only the smudge of orange in the bottom corner, in which the fire is reliably reflected.

~

His advisors panic among themselves, not letting on. They all have promises made to people richer than them at home, to people more powerful than them abroad. They are giving assurances. They are hedging their bets, trying to stay in favour – this might be a slow start, he may yet come round, he may acquiesce. Staying in favour but also perhaps dipping in to conversations about who might be an appropriate heir should the worst happen, should they need to call anyone in from the wings, God forbid and long live the King. Occasionally writing a letter abroad to a bastard or an uncle or the descendant of anyone with royal blood, asking after their health, their coffers, their appetite for a visit to court.

BLACK GRASS

The King, he wakes in the night and thinks, enough of this and how can I escape it. He thinks of his oldest brother dying so suddenly, and being instructed to place his own cheek on his brother's cold, almost-wet cheek and bid him farewell with a kiss, how a child should never have to do that. And he cried silently then, even though being in his brother's presence when he was alive made him feel like the tip of a blade was being drawn lightly across his skin. But all the same, he couldn't believe him dead – couldn't believe a person could so suddenly vacate their body. That it might become a vessel overnight. He thinks of his other brother dying so slowly – being leeched of life, and surely knowing it was coming. Forced to walk all the way down an unbearably long dark corridor. Some nights he thinks on other deaths gone by, and on those yet to come. On his brothers but also on friends from childhood, the one who drowned and now sits at the end of his bed dripping and tinged green. And on his mother, gone so long ago as to almost feel like something he read in a story. But he remembers the feeling of it even if not the event, the feeling hanging in the air so dense you can feel it forcing its way down your throat. Doom. A shadow and no one saying what is happening or why everything is suddenly so frantic, or why no one is answering your questions, and then the news that your mother, she is dead. And you must be brave and not cry in front of anyone – knowing this, even though no one has expressly told you. He found his brother crying in a large cupboard that night, but that was the end of it. His relatives have all left him and he feels in his blood that he must somehow be the cause of it. And now the King finds himself waking at night and before he has time to understand that he is awake and the moon is coming in between the curtains onto his brow or the rain is hammering the window, he is thinking about the death of his wife, who he loves so much, and the death of his cats, and the deaths of his friends who now feel so very far away from him. He imagines the moment of the loss and he imagines his mourning, and all night he weeps for the sadness that awaits him.

ANTS

The young Attendant is called to the King's rooms to assist with packing. Enough garments for three days, maybe four. Silk throws and cushions for the journey. A couple of the lower-value gifts from the dead King's coronation to bestow upon the host.

He knows the order of the King's apartments fairly well, having been invited to keep his company on a handful of occasions now, and from being observant when he is on watch at the door and the senior attendants move about the space. He now knows where they place the fine linens and whence they retrieve the jewels. The young Attendant's wife tells him to be careful – close to a King is a charmed and dangerous place to be. The advisors think it wholly inappropriate – this King is not the first to enjoy the company of his inferiors, and he will not be the last, but to flaunt it before he has secured the love and respect of the court, of his council, well it irks them. He might as well spit in their faces, so little love has he shown them. The rest of the staff make snide comments to the young Attendant as they prepare the King's trunk; they presume he knows where the King keeps his undergarments.

The King and Queen are to visit a Duke in the country. The young Attendant hears him described variously as formidable, very fine, very rich and ungodly. Someone talks of his rumoured bloodline link with an overseas ruler. A ruthless one. The Duke makes regular donations to his cause. From the Queen's maid-of-honour he hears of other things that happen at his residence . . . let it only be said that he prioritises pleasure in them all. The Chief Advisor had decided that it would be good for the King to be reported as seeking the Duke's company. Word of it would reach way beyond court. People might think the King is seeking an allegiance, learning a thing or two about how other countries do things.

The King wants nothing to do with the Duke. Even his brother – pragmatic and strong of stomach as he was, no stranger to readying his troops a few times a year – had found the Duke overzealous in his appetite for conflict, which seemed to bring him more pleasure than all of his other pursuits combined. But the King needs to get away from the palace, needs the quiet of a carriage in motion, with only the sound of the Queen's breathing. Perhaps some birdsong over the crunch of the wheels. This is the only way.

~

Hooves on the cobbles announce the departure of the King, along with the Queen, the Chief Advisor and a few footmen behind them on horseback. Rain hits the court windows. Rain hits the shoulders of the congregated household in the courtyard, lined up to bid their majesties farewell.

~

It is a matter of moments before the mood changes. It is suddenly unusually quiet. As he walks through the corridors, the young Attendant senses a kind of congregating, like ants moving under the earth.

He is beckoned silently, by a member of the King's council, into a room. Told to stand with his back to the door and keep watch. He is not sure what or who for, or why he is to be trusted.

The advisors begin:

Let us speak freely – we find ourselves in troubling times.

The facts as I see them are that there is no heir and the King has yet to ... take up the reins of power.

Indeed, it is not clear if he ever shall.   *Careful, my Lord ...*

I would advise caution in our approach – the country has endured enough turmoil to last ten years.   *We cling on by our fingernails.*

The priority must be the production of heirs.   *If I may, is the matter not a little more urgent ...*

Change, if indeed it must come, should take place when we stand on firm ground.

Who might raise the matter with his Majesty?   Who will check with our Lord that he and the Queen are . . . in one another's company, regularly, of an evening?   If the Queen were not so busy being fucked elsewhere . . .

That their graces both understand the . . . act necessary.

*   That our King . . . Perhaps someone might ask whether he is producing a liquid during their . . .*

It may not be altogether ludicrous to be so . . . thorough.   Perhaps even one of us, one of his dutiful subjects, might watch over . . .   An . . . intimate meeting.

*   My lord, please.*

Not watch . . . preside . . . oversee. And not necessarily with the knowledge of Their Majesties.

*   Well, no, of course not all of us.*

*   It is a delicate matter which . . .*

I'd suggest he who has known the King longest may discuss this with him in private conversation.

*   I hate to disagree, my Lord, but a delicate matter requires the distance afforded by lack of familiarity . . . Perhaps the most recently inducted would be best placed . . .*

I must protest, my Lord, and suggest instead . . .

Perhaps the first action, having given it due consideration, is to verify that the Queen bleeds.

Many do not, or they bleed so much as to have too little life force left within them with which to nourish a child.

My wife says that a woman can fail to bear children by simply wishing it so.

The King, of course . . . he must desire nothing more. *The contentment of his people, which surely he will know is fraying, that is the most important thing to a King. Surely he cares about that . . . above all else . . . surely the same is true of every man . . .*

Call one of the Queen's ladies to us so that we may have our concerns settled.

Who attends her at night? Perhaps also a laundress?

Someone fetch one of the Queen's girls to us. We have one of the King's boys here in the room, and one who knows him better than most.

Boy!

They call to him. He realises in this moment that they see him as a body, entirely empty of mind or conviction, until he is bidden by them.

You!

Pick a girl from the Queen's quarters and bring her here. Choose one who looks . . .

   eager to please . . .   *or quick to cry.*

He nods. He leaves the room, takes a moment to recall which direction he must take to the Queen's apartments. To work out what is happening here, what he has been dragged into.

He turns left, passing the portraits which flank the walls and stare him down. Cold, cold faces. He often wonders, if his fortunes had been otherwise, if he had been born with status, whether his face would also have hardened with the privilege.

~

He stops outside the Queen's door, behind which the frisson of gossip is palpable. He knocks. Silence. He waits. The door opens a crack and the Queen's maid-of-honour halts it at the width of her face. *Yes?* Her hand is on the doorframe. The ladies therein are hushed. He explains, falteringly, that he has been sent by the King's council to summon a lady of the Queen's household for questioning. The maid-of-honour would like to know to which of the Queen's girls they are referring.

He does not know. He has been given no instructions. He remembers only the name of the one who would come every day to ask after the appetite of the former King. He says her name.

The maid-of-honour would like to know what it is they plan to interrogate her about. Not interrogate, replies the young Attendant – I believe they have some questions which are delicate in their subject matter. *I know no more.* He is trying to make his face convey to her that he isn't part of this, that he has no choice. The maid-of-honour narrows her eyes a little, turns her head and calls to the girl in question, who appears briskly, red in the face. He knows instantly that he has chosen badly – she is totally composed, tough, even. And he realises in this instant that this must be why she was the one chosen to come each day to the dying King's apartments, to face the scene, to remain inscrutable on return and to ask the same stupid question over and over.

She walks with her chest out, chatting brightly. She has heard that he is in the King's favour – *lucky boy.* He replies that they have conversed a few times – that he thinks them similar people, albeit the King being a King and he a nobody. He has not said this out loud before, not even to his wife. He wishes he could take it back immediately – he says to her that he did not mean to equate himself with the King, could she kindly forget he said it. After a considerable pause, she observes that she thinks the King must feel very alone. All Kings, but this one in particular.

They walk on in silence. When he says that they are almost there, she stops, looks him dead in the eye and says, *I love the Queen and am faithful to her.* She presses her hair and flattens out her skirts.

They reach the door. Voices float through the fine, dark, varnished wood of the door. They allow themselves a few moments.

Well no one concerned themselves much with the width of the Queen's hips at the time. Her hips were of no concern to anyone but her seamstress until last month . . .

He knocks and pushes the door before a beat has passed. They enter. She bows, he thinks rather half-heartedly.

Nothing to worry about at all, my Lady . . .

The physician simply wishes to enquire after the health of the Queen . . .

Please, tell us of her appetite? And her rest? And how often is she sleeping in her own bed and how often the King's?

And the sheets after the King has visited . . . do they appear to have been . . . used?

And the Queen has her monthlies and . . . bleeds blood? The blood is red?

Does she perhaps ever . . . mutter in her sleep and what might she say?

We would appreciate you taking these enquiries more seriously.

And does the Queen not gossip with you and the other ladies? Never? Forgive me, but I find that hard . . .

She says nothing of other men? She says nothing of her prayers? The requests she puts to the heavens?

It is useless. This woman is a wall. They ask after her husband and children – perhaps if some information might occur to her then they should all find themselves in more fortunate circumstances. She has no husband or children. They say that they pray no unfortunate rumours were to tarnish her reputation – it may not be so easy to secure that husband after all and wouldn't that be a shame. She laughs with a single puff of her nose.

They dismiss her.

They turn on the young Attendant. He made a poor choice – they are incensed.

And you, boy, let's see if you can be any less useless than the mule you dragged to us.

You attend the King at night? And the Queen is often present?

Have you witnessed them ever in coitus? No, I do not mean watched … I mean … Do you hear what you would perceive to be … encouraging sounds when you wait outside?

I'm not suggesting you have your ear to the door, but I think we all know that such enjoyment would be audible to those in the immediate purlieus …

What do you mean by murmurs? Can you be more specific?

That they laugh together and call for wine is not useful information, Sir.

In future, so that you do not continue to waste our precious time, you would be well advised to open your ears . . . and then to come and speak with us.

We can then . . .   *We can then see what we*
can do for you.

TRULY PATHETIC

The King returns from his visit unchanged. Not frothing at the mouth for a bit of conflict. Not clutching at his trousers to bend over the Queen.

What did people expect.

Instead, he speaks of a remarkable flower planted in great swathes in the Duke's garden. It was alive with bees. The flowers were pink – a pink like he'd never seen before – and, when rubbed, the foliage smelled of blackcurrant and mint. Please could someone locate it for him.

LOCKED IN

The early spring bulbs have gone over – rigid, petal-less green stems punctuate the borders of the lavish court garden, giving way to iris and marigold.

The coronation is a month away. His advisors have retreated, briefly, after the Queen set them to organising a festival of games with which to surprise their King after the coronation. At this point they are glad of the break, the shift in focus, having run out of ways they might coax the King into action, although they consider this kind of activity somewhat beneath their station and so set tasks for their inferiors.

~

The coronation is in two weeks, mere days away, tomorrow.

The mood in his rooms as he is prepared is one of hushed reverence, which suits both the King and his attendants. No one really wants this, many are indifferent.

He is bathed, shaved, rubbed with aromatic oils of thyme and lovage, bathed again. Layered in fine cotton, lace, silk. Adorned with hundreds of orange sapphires, set in gold, like the stem of a crocus.

~

Then it is done and he hardly feels it happened.

Nothing is changed. If there was music he didn't hear it, or it moved through his head like a syrup, bypassing his ears. The orb was placed in his hand and he watched his fingers open out like a flower to receive it. Into the other hand someone conveyed the sceptre, which was presumably cold to the touch. Oils, a gold ring bearing the face of something with cobalt eyes, a sword resting its weight, briefly, on his shoulder, something placed at his heels, one hand dipped in water, something on his tongue, many blank eyes looking his way, the Chief Advisor looking, resolutely, to the ground, not muttering the assent necessary at the end of prayer. The sceptre and the orb held aloft in front of him, in his own hands, as if floating – the weight of them imperceptible to the King.

~

The young Attendant and his wife fuck during the coronation, making use of the brief quiet. He almost makes it through without thinking of the dead King in his dying, then, there he is: mouth agape, the black hole of it.

~

Reports of the service float through the court – morphing and writhing on the air.

The King gripped the orb as if it were a skull he wished to crush in his palm. He grew red with fury.

The King shook like a new-born calf, fumbling everything he was handed, his lips trembling like an autumn leaf on the branch.

The Queen had a hopeless, faraway look in her eyes. They were still as a winter lake. She is doomed, they are both doomed – she surely knows it.

THE ICON OF TENDERNESS

The King dreams that his cats wake him with their wailing, then fall silent when he seeks to find them.

They hide behind the heavy purple curtain, the three of them huddled together, shaking their heads, pawing at their faces, as if trying to dislodge something inside.

He takes them onto his lap, one by one, and wipes the insides of their ears with a white cloth. When he removes it, the cloth is speckled with tiny creatures, black and red. The cats lift their heads, pathetic and dying – the creatures move behind the surface of their eyes.

~

The following morning the King does not wish to get out of bed. He asks that any urgent business be held off until the next day.

The air is warm and flies gather at the windows. When he opens his eyes to the room they busy his peripheral vision. He feels they must be entering and lodging themselves in the gaps in the walls and joinery – lining up between floorboards, squeezing into drawers and underneath the mattress. A miniature plague, just for him.

The Queen is sent to his rooms to speak sense to him. He cannot hear it, he can barely open his eyes for more than a few moments, and when he does he appears entirely elsewhere. She orders the King's staff that news of his maladies must be kept to his household only. She implores discretion: *simply say that he has a light fever, will soon recover. It is for the benefit of the court, your families, the country.*

She sees their fingers itching at their sides, betraying the urge to bring them to their smirking mouths, to exit the room in haste to tell the first person they see.

~

A woman is always a mother, even when she is not one. Not a moment's peace from it, so say the Queen's ladies when news of the King's great melancholy washes through the court.

ARE VESSELS NOT FOR CARRYING

The Queen notices that now, when people greet her, they look at her stomach before they look at her face, then raise their eyes, disappointed.

YOU MUST FIND A WAY
TO REMOVE YOURSELF

Some days later.

The King is out of bed. He has been making a poor showing of it – dragging his body to council with slumped shoulders and head hanging. His eyes – they remain without light.

His council – the Chief Advisor in particular – have been holding down their rage for many months. But now it is beginning to rise up in bursts, shooting into their fists, which bang the table, or their mouths, which spit out words which should not reasonably be said to a King. He barely hears them. They are used to all manner of ruler – those who oversee everything, and those who only engage with select responsibilities, but do so with zeal and enthusiasm. They are used to Kings who delegate power, who only want to wear fine clothes, who hunt and eat their way through the court. Occasionally they have been confronted with sheer incompetence, but that is an easy enough ship to steer. Never before have they been met with this combination of insolence and stubbornness – a King blocking all action but refusing to hand over the reins. Do they long for the days when the threat of their heads being rendered from their bodies, although minute, existed?

~

Dinner. Sitting at opposite ends of the table – the King and Queen – candlelight bobbing on the waxed mahogany. A warm day during which they had walked the gardens and fallen into easy conversation about the trees and some new planting, the King shedding tears, silent and constant. Recalling that they used to do this so often, didn't they? And no one watching.

There, in the evening light turning purple, the Queen dismisses their staff from the room. They are gone in a matter of seconds.

The Queen rises from the table, walks to the King, cups her hand to his ear, whispers.

MISTAKE

Each time the King is in want of something he must decide who to ask. Where is the danger? Who may be softer than they appear?

This time, he is led by his nose: smells on the man what he takes to be the vague oil of a rosemary bush. Perhaps, when he has a moment off duty, this man walks the gardens and takes a sprig between his thumb and fingers, rubs firmly, then presses down either side of his beard to transfer the scent. Perhaps he also tries, whenever he can, to get his hands into the ground, to dig his way into another life. The man is also fairly new in the King's service. Not quite firmly on one side or the other of any matter just yet. He is surely somewhat adrift, finding his feet in this place.

He asks to see the man – summons him to the table where he reads, writes letters, reviews endless documents, where he does so little of note. The man knocks and waits. This in itself gives away his uncertainty, his lack of understanding; the King's experienced advisors knock and continue through the door with an almost indiscernible pause, as if the door is little more than water, understanding as they do that courtesy is required, nothing more. That the King has no real authority to refuse anyone in matters of business or diplomacy – he must always be ready to be perceived, like an animal in a cage.

The King calls that he may enter as the door swings open. It is lighter than it looks and a person needs time to get used to the force necessary. This man has never opened this door, likely never seen inside this room. The door bangs against the wall.

The King asks after the man – how does he like living at the palace, the demands of his new role – whose eyes move from side to side, as if waiting for the trick to reveal itself. The King asks after his family. A wife and one daughter. The man's eyes change when he mentions his daughter. She is four years old and loves rolling in the grass, trying to find creatures to pick up and inspect. *If she were a man I think perhaps she would be a great explorer,* he says. *Do you like to read?* the King asks. The man replies that he cannot remember reading anything for many years, other than ledgers, maybe since he read the histories at school. The King replies that he is glad he mentioned the ledgers because he himself lately has been chastising himself for his lack of interest in the records of the palace, in his ancestors. He feels it is time he truly acquaint himself. He wonders if this man might take it as his personal project to assemble for the King the ledgers in instalments. To bring him, say, fifty years a month, in a bundle. Then, casually, as if it is just occurring to him, he says that he recalls, though he may do so incorrectly, that a King not more than four hundred years ago had absented himself from the throne and survived. Imagine! The advisor also recalls, though less the detail of the events but more the way they had been skipped over in his class at school – the master dismissing the King with a wave of disgust, looking like he wanted to spit. No, he remembers that the teacher actually did spit on the ground at his feet. It is also his belief that the King in question did, in fact, lose his head. How the children used the cowardly King's name as an insult in their future games.

Why the interest, if I may ask, my Lord.

No interest. I merely wondered what became of him, but that, it seems, is settled.

The advisor's eyes narrow, they flick towards the door. The King feels his mistake immediately, sure as a sudden nausea. Everyone at court is in someone's pocket.

I will set about preparing the ledgers at once, Your Majesty.

THE COLOUR OF PATIENCE IS GREY

He watches the garden after a downpour.

Leaves heavy with rainwater, flowers occasionally tipping their heads to release their burden.

Everything still besides this intermittent bobbing, everything bearing what it can, until it cannot.

THE APPLE KING

He locates the ledger of the Kings within the stack of manuscripts that has been left on his desk, as requested. It is in four parts.

The Queen asks where it has come from – he cannot bear to confess his misstep, so he says that he is merely interested. She tilts her head, purses her lips. They both know what this means: she is aware of his dishonesty, but will allow it.

Since records began there have been 31 Kings spanning just over four hundred years. Each King has a dedicated section in the ledger, the sections naturally varying in length depending on the duration of the King's reign, his achievements, how worthy of poetry, songs, elegies. Some lived mere months, having come to the throne as children. One King reigned for 44 years, one for 11 days. The reports are mostly glowing – penned immaculately on gilded pages. The Kings seem more god than human.

The King he is looking for, the one they are all taught about in their lessons, has two pages in the ledger. He cannot believe that he tricked himself into misremembering the King's fate, and that he did so through sheer force of will. The inkwork is of the same quality as the other entries, but the borders are afforded no decoration. The entry records the name of the King's father, mother, siblings, wife and one child (who did not survive infancy). It records his nickname – *The Traitor King or, the Apple King* – as well as a summary of his rule and demise.

The Traitor King, also known as the Apple King, ruled feebly, producing no viable heirs or bastards, and having no aptitude for rule, no bravery on the battlefield, no lust for the Queen or other women. On Winter Solstice in his first year on the throne, he saddled a horse in the night and rode West. Upon discovering his abscondment, his advisors gave chase alongside a few assembled soldiers, while the Queen and his inner circle – who remained loyal and silent – were tortured for information. The advisors located the King sitting by a tree in a field, his meagre supplies gone and his horse nibbling happily on the grass. As they approached the King, he threw rotten windfall apples, sticks and wet leaves at his men. They lifted the King from the ground, tied him to a horse and returned the King to court, where word of his pathetic attempt to stave off their weapons with apples arrived before he did, escorted by his men, in chains. He was beheaded for treason three days hence, and his head left on display in the market square for a month, where it was pummelled with apples until chunks of flesh began to loosen from the skull. For years following his rule, visiting envoys – particularly those with a grudge to bear, however historic – would greet the ruling King with a mocking gift of a basket of apples. The shame of it was endured by the court for many years.

May we forget The Traitor King and never see his like again, so it please God.

Later scholars hypothesised that the Apple King was not, in fact, the rightful heir to the throne, but the bastard son of the Queen and her fool, who came from overseas.

VOICES WITH NO
MOUTHS ATTACHED

The King fantasises, before he sleeps, that he is in bed in a country house – the Queen in a nearby room and the cats at his feet. The house is large but not overbearing. Cheerful fires crackle in the grates, a peach-coloured rose spreads like a rising sun across the brickwork. The many trees in the orchard bear fruit and it is his to pick.

~

Elsewhere, in the dark of corridors and in the shade of the gardens, whispers begin to circulate thus:

> *The King is seeking to absolve himself of his duties.*

> *He makes enquiries to people who owe him no loyalty. Idiot man.*

No doubt he has designs to make off in plain sight, to great fanfare, on a horse decked in gold cloth. No doubt he thinks he can get away with anything.

By what authority? By what authority does he believe he may refuse the throne?

What is this if not a direct challenge to the God who chose him to rule.

(By whatever divine insight, we cannot fathom but we must respect.)

God is almighty and all-knowing. Amen.

Is the King not himself blaspheming?

Could we not call the King himself a traitor to the throne?

Could we not call him the greatest blasphemer?

And what would we do, without a second thought, to any other traitor? Any blasphemer?

I make no suggestions, merely present the situation as it stands.

PLANTING

Someone looking in through a crack in the door and into the King's room, and in turn inside the King's own head as he sits at his desk spinning his quill between his thumb and forefinger, would see what the King is thinking.

There are places in the garden's beds that need to be filled. Now is the perfect time – the earth is warming up beautifully. The gaps, the bare ground, are full of possibility. Gums with the promise of teeth. What would I give to be the man pressing the earth down around the roots? The fields will be dotted with lambs, the forest lively with fawns. Would I kill someone, many people, to escape this life and roam?

~

One day he spends an afternoon at his table working at his project. He has his eye on a single rose in the bush by his window. In the morning it is closed. As the sun moves across the flowers it loosens, and each time he looks, it is larger, freer, than before.

SPLASH

Someone looking in through a crack in the door and into the Queen's room (so conscientious are her ladies that such a crack would never exist) would see the room alive with conversation.

There has been a new arrival at court. The wife of the King's cousin, visiting from overseas, quite out of nowhere. They hear that even the King's council are taken by surprise. The cousin himself was raised here, educated alongside the King and his older brothers, afforded near enough the same privileges. There, he bloomed into a sturdy and witty young man, before he was sent abroad for an advantageous marriage, securing the daughter of the King in an allied territory, where he has lived prosperous and charmed ever since, under the protection of a benevolent father-in-law. Now his wife is here, at court, quite unaccompanied.

The Queen – who is always judicious, but loves a little mischief and gossip – is not here to satisfy anyone's curiosity.

The palace staff have heard that the cousin's wife is not used to the customs of their court. The most noble of the King's attendants scrambled to greet her in their finery as she arrived. She shunned their offer of help down from the carriage, and she was not heard to thank them. And it was noted. She barely glanced up from her astonishingly fine shoes as they tapped their way across the cobbles.

The men of the court wonder at length not only why she is here, but why she is here alone, and by what authority, how is it that she dares. Surely, they agree, her husband will follow swiftly, surely she is intended as company for the Queen. They also agree, by the by, that her face is too stern. Her dress more that of a harlot than a King's daughter.

The women are thrilled – they suspect that they will like this fashion.

~

Word flies around the court – the cousin's wife is presently walking in the gardens with the King and Queen. Someone reports that the King was heard laughing. *Has anyone heard this before?* they ask of each other. The King's laugh a blood moon.

It is rumoured that she will dine with the King and Queen the following tonight.

PRE-DRINKS

As the King is shaved and dressed and his hair oiled, there is a new energy about him. He deliberates over his outfit – choosing carefully and asking the opinion of the young Attendant as to whether the green or the blue tunic. Carried away, he makes a slightly garish choice.

~

Someone looking in through the window of the King's bedroom would see nothing but a small fire in the grate, an empty chair at the King's table and a stack of papers gleaming unnaturally white in the flamelight.

The King meanwhile is being conveyed to a large, ostentatiously beautiful room many corridors away. He has dined in this room two or three times in the past – obliged to court foreign emissaries when his father or brother was absent – always utterly baffled by his own presence and purpose at those meals. He had felt that he may as well be a farm animal dressed in fine clothes.

But now, the room is his. It will be used only when he expressly desires it.

He enters and is greeted by a table crowded with meats and fruits, pastries, sweets and pies. Silver goblets and plates, chalices of green glass. Copper and bronze candlesticks luminous with the reflection of flame. The best wine the palace has to offer – opaque like blood. Five silver fish are laid out parallel to one another, alternately top to tail, tail to top, on an elaborately carved platter. A musician is playing – his fingers tracing out a tune as if they are dancing on the strings. Whence has this spectacle appeared, he wonders – and on whose orders.

The Queen enters the room behind him, placing a hand on his lower arm.

DAWN

The next day.

~

The attendants present at the dinner are pulled into shady corners by advisors, nobility, holy men – the people who have their whole hands, not merely their fingers, in as many pies as possible. They are up to their wrists in it all.

What news? What scandal? Who saw her?

No reports. No news. Nothing but low, measured conversation. *A woman, like any other.* This is what the attendants say. And while they have no evidence to the contrary, nothing they can pin down, not one of them believes it. What was it about her? She ate methodically, refusing that which she knew she would not like, even when it had been made specially for her and was presented with an expectant flourish. She did not apologise or blush, she did not placate or praise. She asked many questions. She complained not of the journey or the weather. She drank the wine and asked for more. She looked at the King directly, she touched the arm of the Queen with a firm familiarity. She laughed loudly, and often. Her sleeves were long and adorned at the cuff with large black bows – altogether too much like a man's.

~

The King is up early.

Moving around his rooms with something resembling energy, asking questions of his attendants, about their health, their families, their contentment in his service, the temperature of the room, if it is acceptable to them, whether they might want to take a ride by the stream later since the weather is so mild.

The King has had, not a dream, but a thought that he woke with, long before the sun rose. A rogue thought which, against his instincts, he allowed to enter his mind and which he then nurtured. He pictured his council gathered in a room and, each in turn, approaching where he stood. Terrified and shaking, every last one. Him reaching his arm down their throats and pulling out coins, strings of jewels, fine ornaments. Casting it all out of the window to the poor folk gathered in the courtyard.

The thing is – he is understanding – he could actually do it, owning as he does the bodies of all the realm.

~

Elsewhere, out of sight, a handful of advisors have gathered in a small room. It is a small room that has an unpleasant odour to it, being as it is almost never used and tucked away in the bowels of the council chambers. They resent being forced to meet in this way, with this smell. What are they? Rats at a lump of mouldy bread?

To business. They are here to wonder, merely wonder among themselves, whether the King wishing to abdicate the throne without a named heir – if that is even what the King seeks to do, they themselves could not say, how could they, but he makes enquiries plainly dangerous and sickening about his forebears – would indeed amount to treason. It's a compelling argument, they agree, certainly not one to be ignored. It would leave the throne, after all, wide open for the taking. And when there is something to be grabbed, is it not the most ruthless, the most powerful hand that will seize it? And would there not be much bloodshed, instability, and besmirching of our good name across the four corners of the world?

Then should not we act, should not we do something?

UPRIGHT, ARCHING SPECIES

The paler colours are coming through in the garden now, the lawn is flushing into new growth – green as a tapestry.

When the King takes a walk through his grounds the day after the dinner, he notes the buds tipped with apricot on the climbing rose, the perfection of the bleeding heart, its flowers dangling in an orderly line, juddering in the breeze. He observes the green heads of the peonies, encased so tightly as to appear swaddled. The King recalls the magnificence of the tulips, long since slackened at the neck, which he walked past numbly only weeks before. He recalls too the fuzz of violet-blue on the forest floor, visible beyond the lake he may not circumnavigate alone, and his longing to stand among it.

Those months before, in the immediate wake of his ascension to the throne, he had stood by the lake and looked beyond it to the forbidden ground, carpeted with bluebells. He had looked down at his feet in boots, wet at the tips, and known they would never again carry him where he and he alone wanted to go. His heart thrashed in his breast at the knowledge of it, like a fish held at the gills.

Now, he smells the scent of foliage coming from behind his fingernails, and from his shoulders where the silk of his jacket has brushed the shrubbery of the maze as he walks around it, slowly, towards the centre, where someone else will be waiting to receive him. He looks down at his feet, completely dry, yellow silk with gold brocade at the tip, and is aware suddenly of his toes within them, at the end of his feet, at the end of his legs which can take him wherever he wishes to go.

Deposited back at the palace, he bids the young Attendant invite his cousin's wife once again to dine with him and the Queen. This evening. If it please her.

WEDNESDAY WEED

The King takes to walking the gardens with his cousin's wife each afternoon. A couple of attendants in their wake, straining their ears.

The King wakes, eats, wipes his mouth and dashes the cloth onto the table, attends council, where he refuses to comply, achieving little, aside from enraging his Chief Advisor. The King used to stiffen with terror in his presence, or appear as if drained of blood.

The young Attendant notes that in these last few days the King seems bolstered – as if this situation is a gigantic wave that he has plans to swim beneath.

THIS IS WHAT HAPPENS WHEN A FOETID WOUND IS LEFT TO ROT

An uprising has been rumbling on a nearby island.

It is a historic source of squabbling, like a doll being pulled at the arms between two livid children, where it is the winning that is wanted rather than the doll itself. But that is now all settled – it all belongs to the King's empire.

It has little to offer in resources or men; the people are hungry and weak in winter, scraping by on whatever they can get from the ground and the sea, grateful for the benevolence of the King, for the protection of his wide arms, spread like wings.

It is a nothing place. It was.

All it takes is a handful of people not just interrogating the legitimacy of their situation, but giving voice to that wondering, and doing so in trusted company, then in the market square, then in holy buildings. Suddenly a few questioning mouths become many, and they gather a crowd of people nodding, muttering their assent, shouting for the sharpening of their weapons.

The last King was warned about the discontent of these people; he had plans to meet with their self-appointed leaders. Instead, he died, and the island was forgotten. It was occasionally raised with the new King at council, recently ever more firmly. He did nothing, of course. *We will let them be.*

So, word now reaches court that the rebels have gained numbers and momentum and, worst, the backing of another empire. An empire looking to do what it does best: devour land. Taking the fury of the oppressed and spinning it into gold.

An emergency council is called. The King summoned. Experts in military response and tactics, a couple of holy men sitting by the chill of a window should anyone need to consult God. A large map, replica boats and troops in a chilling, dull metal.

Not ten minutes into discussions, how harassed the King appeared, and trembling slightly when he lifted his cup. Frowning as if burdened by head pain. Surrounded by men with papers, straining at the neck to implore him, to stoke him to violence of a lesser or greater degree.

Burn some houses and holy buildings to send a message.

You need only kill the leaders to put the rest of the population back in its place.

Seize their stores and destroy their crops – it will be done in a matter of days.

Crush them once and for all. Wipe them out. We will find a use for the land.

How appalled they were when he requested that his cousin's wife be summoned at once, horrified by her appearance in the doorway, the audacity of her entering the room without being beckoned in. To sit beside the King. To pick up a document and enquire as to the situation.

Are the people very much disgruntled in your occupation of them? Have they good reason? What of your treatment of them – do you provide …

The council looking everywhere but at the source of these questions.

She is a bodyless voice.

Eyes going over her head, into the corners, out of the windows at the perfect, vibrant lawns.

If we do not act fast, we will lose the land, your Majesty. Maybe worse.

Indeed? she replied. *And why should you not?*

CRUSH

The army is despatched without the King's approval.

The order is given by the Chief Advisor, in the dead of night, involving as few men (mouths) as possible. The people must believe that it was the King's bidding, or there will be chaos.

Darkness had fallen and a rider had been sent with orders to raise the commander of the army from his bed. Long enough before sunrise to ensure that he could not be followed and apprehended by the King, as if the King would have woken up and discovered this betrayal and, enraged, sought to rectify it. As if he would.

No one is sure whether this has happened before. Not simply making decisions on behalf of a King who is too young, old or incompetent – which is done when it has to be – but behaving as if there is no King at all. Certainly not in the memory of anyone living, even the old aides who sleep at the table during council discussions, who have seen five, maybe six Kings. Not even the handful of old women who tend to the births of the nobility. They have seen more bloodshed than all the men at court combined.

But it has happened now, and the King discovers it only when the young Attendant hands him a folded note, as he has been instructed. The young Attendant notes the lack of a waxen seal and thinks the council cowards for it. But the King does not seem to care about the betrayal, only the answer he receives when he asks the Chief Advisor whether mercy will be extended to the rebels.

Your Majesty, they are not people like us. You must bring your head down from the clouds.

~

This great insult to the King's authority must be kept, as much as possible, from the wider court, whose ready lips at the first opportunity will pour it forth into the ears of acquaintances, visitors, absent nobles and staff, who in turn will roll it through the filthy streets of the nearest town. A stick dropped into the young river will eventually wash up on its sludgy banks. But the truth, so scandalous that most dare not believe it, leaks out through the gaps in the Chief Advisor's hands.

He has his message ready: this was ordered by our Lord and master, decisive as he is, and without mercy.

The Queen consults the cousin's wife. They agree, better the King is protected from this information, as much as he can be.

ROASTING

The King, that week, sleeps so well.

A person, by some miracle suspended in the air outside the top-most floor of the palace, and looking in at the window that overlooks the maze, would see the King on his back, one arm flung above his head in abandon.

~

Often, the King dreams he is naked, walking through gardens grown wild and green. His arms are pulling down at his shoulders – a very heavy sword in one hand, a tool for digging in the other. As he walks between high shrubs, spiders' webs catch at his throat. The sword thuds to the ground. He walks on. Before long he feels the weight of the webs slowing him, the not-unpleasant pressure coaxing him to a stop. He wakes aroused.

~

He finds the energy, the conviction, perhaps it is even a compulsion, to tell his Chief Advisor that another betrayal, another use of his army without his explicit command, and he will have his life as easily as a gardener snips the spent head off a rose. The Chief Advisor is shocked to find that he almost believes it.

~

The King had been appearing to sink, but now he is rising up to the surface, as if pulled by a line.

THIS OR THIS

Behind a large ornamental hedge, one noble passes into the ear of another a story about the King and his young Attendant. The young one with the wife who works in the nursery. A sordid little story that it brings him no pleasure at all to be sharing.

Rumour is that, while innocently walking through the gardens, the Queen's maid-of-honour chanced upon a window – a beautiful window shaped like an almond – and framed in that window was the young Attendant leaning back upon a table, cock in the mouth of the King, who knelt before him on the floor. What was she to do, in her shock, but run to the other ladies and tell them what she had seen in great detail – how the young Attendant had his eyes closed and his mouth open while the King was looking up at him, imploring. That they were fully clothed, the King all in blue with the embroidered knees of his britches so uncouthly fretting the gleaming floor. That the young Attendant, in moving a hand, knocked to the ground two or three papers, that when he made to pick them up, the King held him firm by the hips. That she turned and ran as soon as she saw it. Actually, she stopped to watch, but only incredibly briefly, or perhaps for a time, just to be sure. Frozen to the spot.

The ladies lap it up like milk. Some share the story with whichever person they first encounter in the corridor, some wait to tell husbands or lovers, or an acquaintance to whom they desire to appear more interesting.

But some wonder, had this scandalised maid-of-honour not lied to them all before about securing the affections of a Duke who was shortly due at court? And did he ever arrive and were they ever wed? Evidently not. And does that window not face all manner of shrub and small tree whose reflections could very feasibly morph and manipulate a person's imagination? Someone reflects that surely council was convened that morning. Was the King not sitting in a circle with his advisors at that hour, no doubt crying?

[   ]

The King is becoming expert in wasting everyone's time.

Inaction, inaction, inaction.

He cares little.

~

No, he will not come when called. He is no dog.

Was that not a smile, albeit a stifled one, from the young Attendant with whom he converses privately when he can? Is he not enjoying this spectacle – the King digging his hooves into the mud?

REFRESHMENT

The young Attendant to the King, along with everyone else, notices the sustained change in their leader. Gone is the constant expression of woe, or fear. It is not that he now makes decisions or issues commands, but rather that he is assertive in his refusal. He will not cooperate.

For example, one day the young Attendant is conversing with the King. The King is speaking of his earliest memory – that of a foreign ruler visiting court and being greeted by his father. They stood in a line to welcome their guest – his father first, then his oldest brother, then his second brother, then him. How he loved it, being able to observe the man as he spoke with them each in turn, how those feelings changed to panic when the foreign King reached him and knelt down in front of him to extend his hand in introduction.

Then one of the other attendants arrives at the King's door, tells him that the Chief Advisor requests a meeting. The King, without pause, says, *Tell him no, please.* He returns to his story, leaving the poor attendant standing in the doorway, quite at a loss.

The young Attendant is enjoying the King's display. He is willing him on.

He notices the King noticing his smile and reddens at his shamelessness.

~

The rumours, naturally, are that the King has taken his cousin's wife to bed, and that consequently she has bewitched him in this way. But the young Attendant has had the night shift of late and knows that the King remains in his chambers, and that no one visits besides the Queen. Unless they are fucking in the gardens in plain sight, or in her quarters, which is not beyond a possibility. He has heard talk of secret passageways linking the King's rooms to other parts of the palace. It could be true. But the King also seems to him a tactful man – and cautious, too. He has never asked for a man or woman to be delivered to him.

GETTING WHAT YOU WANT
WHEN YOU WANT IT

Someone looking in through the King's window – the small square window, set deep into the wall and covered at almost all times with a curtain of crimson velvet – would see the King alone, sitting at the foot of his bed. Bare feet, white gown hitched up to the waist. His hand at his cock and his face tipped towards the ceiling in raptures.

~

Lately, the King feels that his ears and eyes stretch further. Like after a storm.

MY LORD

The cousin's wife and the King take their afternoon meal together almost daily.

There comes a knock at the King's door, which is promptly opened. Sometimes she is announced by his men but more typically she calls out herself, or over the top of their pronouncement.

My Lord.

Clear as a bell.

And off he goes like a seed into the wind or a rabbit to a trap or a person to the bed of their lover, reclining.

Often, the Queen joins them and they remain at the table for hours. The cousin's wife puts in requests with the kitchen – sweet biscuits with black pepper, meat roasted with salt, cinnamon and orange, fennel seeds coated in sugar.

She gets whatever she wants, for the King requests it, and he eats it all up.

~

The King is writing a letter of many pages at his desk.

Through the window, a peacock in the gardens trembles its feathers into a fan – dazzling emerald green, azure eyes. This is all for the peacock's mate, thinks the King, the peacock cannot even turn its head and see what it has done. It may only see its actions reflected in the eyes of its would-be lover. He finds that beautiful.

He signs the letter, folds the papers, and stamps it with his seal. He stands up, walks to his bed, and places it beneath his pillow.

FIRESIDE

The young Attendant hears much. He hears from a young, flushed servant of the kitchen that the King and Queen fornicate with the cousin's wife all day, in plain sight, pausing only for wine and to tear some meat from a bone. Someone also tells him that they pretend to be animals, the King and Queen, and the cousin's wife plays the goatherd, the stable boy or the monarch posing for a portrait with them on the floor at their feet. The King with his cock out like a dog, the Queen panting all the while. He relays this to the lady-in-waiting, who appears unbothered by her previous summoning to the council for questioning at his hands. He is sure to keep a questioning tone in his throat when he relays the rumour, but she laughs in his face, loudly.

~

The young Attendant hears from his wife, who spends her days tending to the noble children of court amid the wet nurses and tutors, that the cousin's wife has been sent here to entrap the King on the orders of her husband, that he may slip in and have the throne while she rides her lover.

~

The young Attendant wakes and takes his shift at the King's door. He is told by his fellow attendant – who heard it from the attendant he relieved from duty mere hours ago – that last night, or perhaps the night before, the King was troubled again and called for his cousin's wife. It is becoming his habit, they all hear.

She was sleeping – the knock entering her dream as the hammering of her father's knuckle on the table at dinner, and then as the tapping of a large bird at the window, falling into synchronisation. Father and bird. She woke, looked to the window for the beak, the puffed chest. Realised her mistake, settled into her surroundings, knew already what the request would be. All this she told her confidante the next day. She threw a robe about her shoulders and assured the boy at the door sent to summon her, *Yes, yes I am coming.*

And here the boy's account kicks in again: she moved slowly, thoughtfully, fully awake. She tied the cord at her neck in a bow, undid it and re-tied it more neatly. She said, *If he is troubled now he will still be troubled in an hour.* The boy sensed something in her tone – was it disgust? Malice? The cousin's wife followed behind the boy. She told him that she always enjoys her walks to the King's chambers – they allow her to study whichever boy is in front of her – to better understand the fashions and customs of this strange court. She notices where the hair sits on the neck, the length –

if there is any – of the facial hair. It is a short walk through dim corridors but she takes it slowly.

The King was sitting fireside, one arm to his forehead, thumb and middle finger pressing lightly at his temples, the other resting on his thigh. He looked like a painting of a King, were Kings ever permitted to look anything but absolutely sure of themselves. Were they allowed to display such a plebeian weakness as desiring warmth. The King apologised to the cousin's wife once the door was closed (the attendant continued to watch through the crack, to listen with a cupped hand). Then, the King began to cry. She moved to his chair, stood behind him and placed the palm and fingers of one hand flat against his chest, while the other she rested on his shoulder. She has learnt the ways to comfort him. A palm against the heart. The act always reminding her of her friend soothing his baby in this way, laying his hand, almost the size of the child's whole torso, on her body and rocking her gently from side to side. The baby has since died and she cannot look at her friend's hand without seeing the baby, can't imagine the baby in the ground without the hand there also. (All this she told her confidante, but was overheard by the maid-of-honour.)

She allowed the King some time. The fire crackled, with white hot eyes in places. He wiped the tears with his wrists and made a sound to signify that he was done with crying. That he was sick of it. He took her hands in his, asked if she had been sleeping. She said she had.

The King took a finger on her right hand into his mouth. The boy was shocked by this flip in the King's mood. A lifetime of his every whim being accommodated, he supposed, never needing to suppress an urge, the glass being filled before you have realised you are thirsty. Was it envy he felt as he watched? If it was, he did not say.

The King asked *Will you help me sleep*, pressed her hand with its wet finger to his forehead. She faced him, sat astride him, lifted his shirt. Kissed him on the mouth, on one side of his neck and then the other, and back to the mouth. Took his hand, placed it underneath her and moved back and forth on his fingers. She did everything slowly, making him feel attended to, and the expression on his face was bliss, like a cherub. She lifted her robe over her head. Reached down to the King's trouser buttons. It will be quick. It always is when he has been lost inside his thoughts and returns to the world so suddenly like this. He is greedy then. (So says the confidante.) She held him right at the entrance of her, not letting him in. He gripped the arms of the chair and leaned back a little. They both seemed to enjoy this purgatory. (The attendant at the door hardly dared breathe.) She made him say *Please*. Not just once, but again, and then again. And one more time.

When does a King ever ask anyone for anything?

The people of the court burn as they share this story – it spreads like ink in water.

PUPPET SHOW

The troops have arrived on the island – the nothing place.

Once their oars had hit the water there was no calling them back, so they are camped on the southernmost point of the perimeter, their ships undulating out of sight behind the rocks, the men barely concealed by scant shrubs and small trees. The nights have a brutal chill, and they are tearing through supplies, waiting for the command to attack. It is no longer a command the Chief Advisor can give. He thought the glade was clear to canter through, but now there is a stream, and suddenly he cannot cross.

The King orders mercy for the rebels. Retreat. No one will die on his command.

It is the only order he has ever given, the only time he has appeared to care about anything. His advisors are taken aback. The Chief Advisor is incandescent. This can only mean disaster for his reputation. He will lose the heart of the army. He will be crushed.

They cannot disobey the King.

One advisor, told so by his wife, who has been taken into the confidence of the cousin's wife, reports that it is all that harlot's doing. That the cousin's wife advised the King: *Let your army seize their weapons. Let them bring the leaders back here for questioning. It will spare the soldiers some humiliation. It will appease the council. You can hold the rebels here for just long enough that everyone forgets, then send them home. It is no more than a game.*

The King concurs.

~

Up start the mouths again:

By what string is the King manipulated?

> *The wooden crossbar surely jiggles in the hand of the cousin's wife, who makes the King nod yes and shake no and stomp his foot to the ground.*

> *(What she is doing with her other hand we dare not wonder.)*

> *With one hand she holds the wooden crossbar that manipulates the strings, and in the other she tugs at the King's cock, making him nod yes and stomp his foot to the ground.*

186

Beyond the strings and beyond the hand at the wooden crossbar is an arm and beyond that a whole body.

To whom does the arm belong, the arm beyond the hand? And to whom does the body belong, the body beyond the arm? In what room does it sit? How gilded?

The body cannot be hers. A woman could not. Her husband, the King's cousin, surely wears her like a glove.

The body sits in a room in a castle across the sea, and atop that body is a head, and that head is empty for want of a crown.

THE LORD'S OVEN

The Chief Advisor has been bested this time, and knows it.

When the troops are returned to home soil he will do what he must. He will ensure that they know by whose hand they have been rendered so useless.

~

He is granted an audience with the King, eventually. May he be so bold as to join his Majesty, the Queen and his cousin's wife at their next supper? He fears he has not shown her the welcome she deserves, daughter of a King as she is.

He may not. He is excused.

ONE SEASON BECOMES ANOTHER

The alliums come and go, giving way to the foxgloves and lupins.

~

The young Attendant hears that the Chief Advisor and the cousin's wife have dined together privately. They ate venison and egg tarts dyed with saffron.

Should he bring this to the attention of the King? He asks his wife for counsel. *Stay back, my love,* she says, *You grow too familiar.*

GLAIR

It is almost warm and the King is at his table, getting on with things, eating pretty well, planning his great project; it is the plan he sees each time he sits by the fire and loses his thoughts in the flames.

He discovers that he is finding particular pleasure in the purple sweets of lavender, and in a jewelled pile of pomegranate seeds tumbling off a small white plate, in cinnamon cakes the size of a single bite. Small joys punctuate the yawning discomfort of his situation – this is how he is learning tolerance.

The King asks his young Attendant one day how the cinnamon cakes are made, realising he lacks any and all knowledge of the creation of one food from what he assumes is many ingredients. He is told flour, which as his Majesty knows is made from the grinding of grain and appears like a powder, sugar or honey, he cannot be sure which, eggs, and a spice which he believes in its original form looks like a branch of a tree. The King must know more – he is to be conveyed to the kitchens and shown. The cook, astounded by the sudden appearance of his Lord, abandons the crude joke he is telling the spit boy, and wipes his hands frantically on his apron. The kitchen falls quiet, heads are bowed. *The King wishes to see the making of the cinnamon cakes* – this from the young Attendant who with a jolt realises he is to be the handler of the situation. The King is shown flour in a large bowl, which he pokes at tentatively with his little finger. So soft. The cook demonstrates how he takes an egg, cracks its thin shell on the side of the bowl, deposits it in the well in the flour. An egg is placed in the King's palm at his request, the King who has never before touched an egg. He observes it from many angles, rolls it back and forth. He takes his eye from his hand to pay attention to the jar of honey he is being shown – *Is it not the colour of flame*, he says – and the egg falls to the floor. It falls and, perfectly intact, begins to roll purposefully to the feet of the young Attendant. The cook declares it a wonder. *Does not our King have the very hands of God?*

And so the story of the King's small miracle spreads.

~

Then, weeks disappear in a blink. It is hot and he is at the table, sweating, writing letters. Receiving his council and attending to his duties with a reluctance that resembles a child being forced to step into a too-cold bath to endure a scrubbing.

He will sign off what he absolutely must, he will receive foreign guests who insist on visiting court, he will consider trade deals to avoid war. He keeps the country in a sort of stasis, like a yolk suspended in its clear jelly. He knows that, given the chance, many of his advisors would break it with a sharp jab of the finger.

They must be making their own plans, in secret, in the recesses. He is no idiot. He knows how men work.

~

The cousin's wife has remained at court but the heat of her presence has cooled, and chatter about her – and what she is to the King – has died down. It is no thing of note, after all, for a man to be bewitched by fucking. There is only so long news of their coupling can sustain the appetites of the court, then it is on to the next thing. Given that the King is evidently indisposed, will the Queen try to produce an heir with any attendant who bears a resemblance, instead? Is the King himself orchestrating it? Does he watch on from the corner of the room as the Queen takes them on, one by one?

One day, some noble might reminisce about the coronation: *Remember how the harlot's hands twitched when first she saw the crown? She dribbled down her chin with lust for it.* And their companion might counter that they are sure the cousin's wife had not yet arrived at court when the coronation took place. Someone else might agree, someone else might not. And so on, they will continue, until their lip catches on a new line.

~

The salvias are in flower. Pink like radish, pink like strawberry jam, pink like raspberry, pink like guava flesh the King has no knowledge of.

DO WE DEBASE OURSELVES SO?

It is said that the King and Queen have between them taken so many lovers that they must now convene them in the apartments shared by the Queen and her physician, not dissimilar to chickens in a coop.

Everyone knows, everyone believes it in their heart to be true, even when the lady-in-waiting says *No, you will find not a soul in there save our Queen at her embroidery.*

The Head Gardener swears he saw in through a window, newly exposed after he had pruned the wisteria. The people in the room were draped over one another, like slugs on young plants after rain. He could make it all out through the thin cotton of the summer curtains, even in such brilliant light.

DINNER

The Queen, the King and his cousin's wife are convened for their supper.

A person attending to their wine and removing their empty dishes would note how they are discussing the business of the day. The Queen reports that a new spice has arrived at court which the emissaries say goes incredibly well with roast pig. They drink wine. And what strange custom has his cousin's wife learnt about their court this day, for there is always something new. The cousin's wife reports news from home, of her husband, talks of what she misses. The King declares that he has a great love for his cousin, that his childhood was the richer for his presence.

After the meal, the King announces to his staff that they may go – this is perfectly usual.

~

Someone hiding in the trunk in the corner, catching a sliver of the room through a crack in the side, would see their three heads lean towards each other, like swans in greeting. Then, fervent, low muttering.

OFFICINALIS

The King's advisors, or more specifically those most disgruntled and, so, keen to huddle together in dank rooms, appear to have made little to no progress any which way.

On the one hand: the King makes no further enquiries that cause them alarm. Instead, he and his harlot seem to spend time together quietly and without controversy. If they were plotting something, it surely would have been executed by now. Would it not? And there is no sign of her husband, the King's cousin – not even a visit. The King does not behave like a mad tyrant, does not lose battles (for there are none), does not burn through the royal coffers. He bestows no favours, titles or riches on his inner circle. While wounding to them personally and financially, this is hardly grounds for a coup.

On the other: what are they to do, when he will not be counselled, will not take advice? Is content to let any and all opportunity for growth, for glory, pass by. They are made redundant. It is an affront to the general order. It stings. How many years can the country tolerate this, sustaining itself on scraps, while falling in line behind a King it cannot even see? The discontent will multiply like mice in the walls. Neighbours will sniff out their weakness. They must surely act.

REPLICATE REPLICATE REPLICATE

The young Attendant has the night shift again. Through the closed door, he hears the King, alone in the room, talking aloud as if giving a speech to the council:

My lords, I see no just cause to condemn these rebels. I see no need for bloodshed when we may speak and better understand one another.

Then, he is stuck on one part, repeating it and rephrasing it, growing agitated and then steadily louder:

Are we not isolated and inward-looking? Are we not stifled?

Are we not isolated and inward-looking? Are we not choking ourselves?

Are we not self-obsessed and deluded? Are we not stifled?

Are we not stuck and alone? Are we not waking up each day and walking backwards?

Are we not stuck as if in mud, in our own violence? Are we not stagnant?

Are we not in great need of great change? Are we not tired of theft?

Are we not isolated and inward-looking? Are we not stifled?

The young Attendant allows the words to enter his ears and then leave unimpeded, knowing as he does that the King would wish no one to hear them.

ARE WE NOT MANY FISH IN A POND?

It is night. The conifer at the window, were it able to see as with the human eye, would observe the King sitting at his table.

He is alone. He is wearing a loose-necked white shirt, and is writing frantically. When he leans forward to replenish his ink, the shirt gapes slightly, revealing a short stretch of collarbone and his upper chest.

He has so many thoughts in his head, all speaking at once.

It is a wonderful malfunction.

VULGARIS

The next day, a person sitting at the King's table in his vacated chair, as if they were playing the part of him, looking out onto the gardens, would see: the King, the Queen and the cousin's wife walking a path flanked by linden trees.

They stop beneath the conifer – the King leans on the trunk of the tree with his left hand. The cousin's wife has her back to the window – the sun is radiant on her hair. The Queen's lover is nearby, pretending to inspect an oregano plant which grows abundantly between the roses.

~

The Chief Advisor hears from his wife that evening, as they undress for bed, a fresh report circulating among the noble ladies of court.

The cousin's wife took a turn about the rose garden in a dress with unusually large skirts. All who saw it noted how extraordinarily capacious they were. Still, somehow she strolled about quite naturally – albeit, upon reflection, remarkably slowly. She bid a servant cut her a rose – pure white, the centre tightly clustered and the outer leaves lax, louche – which she swung back and forth at her side, pincered between her thumb and forefinger. Taking rest at a small table under a tree, with two accompanying chairs, she sipped on a little wine and nibbled on sugared sweets. Nothing out of the ordinary. Then, did someone not notice the slightest movement beneath her skirts, as when a mouse flits beneath a discarded sack in the grain store? The cousin's wife continued sipping and nibbling, observing the pleasing view from beneath the shade of the tree. She remarked upon it to a nearby lady. Then, did not the underside of the tip of a shoe poke out from beneath the hem of those skirts, and was it the underside of the tip of a shoe so fine that it could belong to no one other than the Queen herself? A beautifully made shoe – one of a pair that her maid-of-honour verified she was wearing later that very day. The servants looked straight ahead, acknowledging nothing. The cousin's wife hid her flushing face in the folds of the rose.

WARNING

The maid-of-honour, who told the story of the King on his knees, sucking on his young Attendant's cock like a lamb at the teat, is watching the Queen and the cousin's wife taking tea together. She has placed a tray of pastries in front of them, poured their wine, asked is there anything else she could do for them and then, when told no, taken her place at the edge of the room. She is on hand, like a piece of furniture that also happens to have a brain and a heart.

~

The Queen had said to her, one morning when the rumour was at its peak, *I hear you have taken a great interest in my husband the King.* Before a response had started forming in her mouth, the Queen had touched her cheek gently, smiled and left the room.

~

The pastries she has served them are the size of plums – iced pale green, with a lace of pink flowers about the rim. They are finer than anything the maid-of-honour owns (this is fundamentally untrue, but she feels it to be so), and there they are nibbling them and placing them down again, unfinished. They barely notice them.

There is something in the look between them that betrays a deep knowing. What could it be? Desire? A dark and terrible secret? Why so hushed, why so much touching of one another's hands and the strip of wrist below the sleeves of their dresses? She will note every movement, every glance, think how to bring them to life in the retelling.

~

When she is standing idle like this, the maid-of-honour allows herself, on occasion, to indulge in something of a fantasy:

She is walking the palace when she comes to a beautiful door of the darkest sycamore wood. A beautiful door so glossed with lacquer that it appears mirrored. The three of them – the King, the Queen and the cousin's wife – are behind it, sitting at the beautiful table of varnished sycamore wood, so long that it would seat sixty. She strains her ears and picks out a fourth voice, low and gentle. The Assistant to the Royal Physician. So, it is the four of them in there: everyone with their lover, everyone with a secret hand somewhere under the table. The four of them sitting at one end, huddled like birds in a nest, bathed in the light of so many candles, picking at platters of the most elaborate pies and sweets and cured meats and roast pig in the new spice. No doubt the Assistant to the Royal Physician reaches towards a platter of painted, shining marzipan fruits – he wears a single ring of onyx and his nails are short, very clean. The Queen reaches for a miniature pie, filled with duck and berries, egg washed to glowing. The fingers of this hand, the left, are adorned with small jewelled rings which dazzle in the candle-light – they are mostly emeralds and sapphires. The cousin's wife holds a little silver knife, its handle engraved with a scene of bathing water nymphs, which she directs towards a platter holding a gleaming pig's head broiled in onions and sage. The King, both hands dotted with pearls and topaz, holds between them the claw of a lobster – so unnaturally, vividly pink it appears orange – which he cracks decisively. He places the claw on his plate and, using a little silver fork, its handle intricately carved with a scene of two ships in battle, drags out the white meat from within. They each take a small bite from their chosen item and place the remainder on their plate. They repeat this process, working their way through the many platters, overflowing with sugared fruits and pastries and knotted loaves and fish, their bellies sliced and splayed, the flesh within the palest pink. The maid-of-honour knocks and enters. They are delighted to see her, bid her join them at once. She sits between the King and the Queen and they pass her exquisite morsels, one after the other, telling her she must try everything. The Queen begins to pleasure her under the table as the King kisses her neck, takes her breast into his mouth. When she is sated and can eat no more, she takes the platters down to the kitchens, where the staff gather and eat what is left. Toothmarks on toothmarks, a little saliva from one mouth into another, carried on a bit of pastry, no bother. They eat their work and they delight that they too have sampled what the King and the Queen and the harlot and the Queen's lover have sampled. They hate them with every bite they take, that they must be grateful for their waste, but there is a thrill in it. Most of all they love the maid-of-honour for bringing them this food, for making this possible.

When her mood is darker – and this happens more than she would like – she knocks and enters and they laugh at her presumption to step a foot into the room. Who does she think she is, they enquire, and what does she think she can offer them? Then, she is walking towards the table at pace, snatching a meat carving knife from an attendant's tray so quickly and without thinking that she perceives it in her hand only for the most fleeting moment – has no idea how it got there – before she is plunging the blade into their necks and backs. When they are all dead, or rendered motionless and bleeding out, she pulls out a chair and sits. The feast is sprayed with blood, so the kitchens prepare her fresh plates, which are presented to her reverently by the servant boys. They love the maid-of-honour for granting them this freedom, for making this possible.

CLEANSED IN AGONY, TINGED WITH JOY

The King moves swiftly through a windowless corridor, in a part of the palace a King has no business being, accompanied by his young Attendant. Their shoes connect with the flagstones in perfect unison – to the ear they are one person.

Barely are they out of sight – slipped off down a lesser-used hallway which, via narrow stairs, leads to the King's chambers – than another door opens. From it, furtive, emerge four members of the King's council. They freeze, sensing movement in the air. They wait.

Who passed here? they ask of each other, their eyes wild. *Spirit or man?*

AUTUMN

The King dreams:

In his garden, one rose is absolutely perfect, like a cup. He wants to cut it down and take it back to his rooms, but knows he cannot. A wave of dog roses with savage, tiny spikes appears, carpeting the lawns, the maze and the paths.

The King is trying to walk across it, to the boundary of the palace grounds, with no shoes on his feet. It is agony, his feet bleed. He shouldn't be able to keep going, but he does.

He is doing it.

THE ICING ON THE

The court wakes to a bright autumn morning – the first frost.

The young Attendant to the King would have nothing of note to report, until a member of the council enters the chamber and demands that he exit at once. In files another, then another after him, and many more entering at something that resembles more a run than a walk, until the council in its entirety has assembled. As he leaves the room, someone calls after him to ready some horses at once, to go directly to the stables and make sure it is done.

Then, muttering so low is it almost imperceptible to his pressed ear:

> *rooms checked*   *the Queen also*
>
> *gardens*   *horses accounted for*   *we must act immediately*

tracks in the mud?   *someone must have*

her lover   *what have you heard*   *unaccounted for*

last seen?   no one knows   missing   send word to country estates

where is the harlot   how must we act?   in what direction? speak up, man,

god

bring the guards who man the gates   *bring the stable boys*

a king cannot simply disappear bring the women who tend to the Queen

shut their husbands in the cellars   check for missing cloaks and boots

beds cold   the harlot, where is she?

On his way to the stables, taking the long, curved route of the path at the edge of the lawn, he stops to admire a single frosted leaf, silver as a fish in the low sun.

WE ADMIT WE HAD BEEN WAITING FOR SOMETHING BUT NOT THIS

Later, the young Attendant is stationed with some urgency outside the King's rooms.

Two advisors take watch inside the King's chambers. One lifts the lid of the large, ornately carved trunk at the foot of the bed. It is full. He lets the lid fall. The other circles the perimeter of the room, slowly, running his finger occasionally along a windowsill as if checking for dust. Opens the wardrobe and peers inside.

~

The members of the council move like rats, as if looking for a prize crumb they have collectively misplaced.

THE HOLE WHERE
THE BULB IS PLANTED

The King is out riding – taking in the fine weather.

The King is at his pleasure elsewhere.

The King is resting with a light fever.

The King is presently unaccounted for.

The King is missing, at this moment.

No one is saying gone.

No one is saying the King is gone.

CONVECTION RAIN

Men on horses leave and return hourly during daylight. The sounds of their hooves on the cobblestones are all but constant. For two days they leave in sets of four – riding out into the rising sun or the high, urgent sun, or the setting sun – and return chilled, or sweating, or soaked through from when the sky broke, unexpectedly. In the hallway, there is a window which affords a view out onto the courtyard they must ride through to reach the stables. From here the young Attendant watches. From here the lady-in-waiting watches.

~

The palace is so quiet.

~

The Chief Advisor paces the corridors, the council chamber, the courtyard, the gardens. To one person he looks like a man with his chair pulled out from beneath him; to another, he appears utterly satisfied.

THE NARROW PATH

The lady-in-waiting hears that the King was poisoned at dinner – that they dragged his gurgling body into the courtyard in the pit of night, strapped it to an unbridled horse and conveyed him deep into the woods, where he was burned, possibly still alive. That the Queen, being loved as she was, was done the honour of a single blade to the heart. That she fell silently to the ground like a robe being shucked off, as if she understood. The lady-in-waiting hears that this was the work of the Chief Advisor, that it was many months in the plotting. As soon as the last King grew weary and had upon him the look of death, the plan began to tap away at the eggshell of his skull. That the cousin's wife was brought to court by him, and by her hand and her body the King was encouraged to sanction just enough that his cousin's troops could be assembled. That the King signed whatever she asked, without even reading. That it was all so easy, the two of them pushing King and council back and forth like a paper boat on water. But had anyone actually seen the Chief Advisor in the company of the cousin's wife? Had anyone heard them exchange words, even? Was there not usually a great distance between them? Either way, the lady-in-waiting hears that the cousin will take the throne, and that he will be met with no resistance. That he will be a real King, and one that the Chief Advisor can animate. There is then no height to which he cannot rise.

The young Attendant to the King hears that the King and Queen, along with her lover, fled in the night – slipping through the grounds on foot, meeting tethered horses on the far side of the lake. That they rode silently to the coast, where they met a ship, and that from that ship descended the King's cousin, hand extended in benediction. He hears that the King, the Queen and her lover boarded the ship, while the King's cousin mounted the horse. The switch was as easy as that. The council had less than no idea – they have been taken by surprise as much as the court to find themselves sitting in the palm of a new King, who will arrive here in a matter of hours or days. He hears that the paperwork was all arranged by the vanished King – new laws had been passed granting the monarch the infallible right to abdication and the appointment of an heir. That at least two of the council would have been in on it, helping the King to navigate the doctrines and laws, and that it was all done under the nose of the Chief Advisor, who was played for a fool by the King's performance of ineptitude. No one asks the young Attendant what he knows.

A variation on the theory heard by the young Attendant, being given credence and much parade by the Queen's maid-of-honour, is that the Queen's lover did not flee with them, although he helped with arrangements. This was to be the Queen's great sacrifice. She left in the dead of night, alongside the King, and was heard to emit a single howl as they crossed over the palace's borders and into the

215

lanes beyond. People thought it a wolf. The maid-of-honour heard it herself. Where, then, is the Assistant to the Royal Physician now? Flitting about court, same as everyone else, or otherwise locked in a secret room, weeping for his loss. Where are the King and Queen, according to the lady-in-waiting? *Running*, she says, just *running*.

The Physician, finding himself unable to locate his Assistant, believes that this was all the work of the Queen. That she set in motion this takeover by way of suggestion, in collusion with the cousin's wife. That she has escaped now with her lover, the two of them parting ways with the King halfway into the woods, never to see him again. Or that – is it beyond the realms of imagination? – she arranged to have the King killed after they fled, him having believed that the three of them would make a new life together, her having very different ideas. Truly, it is entirely possible that she never loved the King at all – women are, after all, famed for their powers of tolerance. How long had she been pulled down by the weight of this man, how utterly tired of him she must have been.

The council mostly believe that the cousin's wife, over these many weeks, by way of lewd and salacious activity – activity which knew no bounds of decency or godliness – manipulated the King so thoroughly that he agreed without thinking to her proposal. That she promised to make his worries disappear like a vapour. The daughter of a King, after all, can be as ambitious as any man. With brothers blocking the way to the throne of her own country, she created for herself a new and eminently walkable path. She will now slip into the role of Queen as easily as putting her feet into fine silk slippers. In time, her husband, the King's cousin, will rule by

216

her side. His claim is as legitimate as any – the people will accept it – but hers will be the voice and the vision. Hers will be the fist.

The Chief Advisor is oddly quiet, refusing to align himself with this theory, or any other. He repeats variations of phrases which declare this to be a situation quite without precedent, quite the shock to them all, imploring people to keep their heads, counselling patience while they seek to better understand what has happened, what on God's earth has happened. Does he flounder, the council wonder, having finally found himself called to steer the ship? Others say that a man without questions is the man who has all the answers.

WITH BRONZE AS A MIRROR

The court – congregated in the larger rooms of the palace, some in corridors, some in basement rooms, huddled as if sheltering from a storm – believe that, were the King alive, he would surely have sent word to reassure them of his safety, that this was all his plan. Silence can mean nothing but that the King is dead, or imprisoned, along with the Queen, for it is unthinkable that any King would vanish on his people. But, if so, murdered or imprisoned at whose hands? The council's or the King's cousin's?

If the cousin's, then should not the council assemble the army against him at once? Surely his troops are on their way to court as they speak, to enforce order, and perhaps cut down those who have risen too high? Should someone not keep watch for men on horseback in the palace courtyard?

If the council's – if they have put an end to the King's rule, spitting in the face of God – does not the very order of their lives now have no meaning? Whence will retribution come?

~

The stable master makes for the vaulted chambers – where many of the lesser families have gathered – at great pace. He announces that the King's horse has been found many miles away by a farmer, nibbling the grass alongside his flock, and without a rider.

A member of the Queen's household runs to the ladies convened in her chambers, relays breathlessly that the cousin's wife, the harlot, was mere moments ago seen fleeing the maze at an unholy pace, almost as if her feet did not touch the grass beneath her.

In the great hall, an attendant keeping watch from one of the windows facing the woods cries out that troops approach, great in number, moving like shadows between the trees. A fellow attendant appears at his side, asks are they not simply the flies which have gathered above the lawn these past few weeks, hanging like clouds and bothering the ladies? The first attendant says no, he would swear on the holy book that he saw troops, that they are coming.

The birds in the aviary are agitated – flapping and moving from perch to perch.

In the kitchens, hands dip into sacks of almonds, biscuits are conveyed into pockets, a large pie is portioned and shared. The serfs chatter easily among themselves, sitting in rows at the perimeter of the great hall, eating what should have been the royal household's morning meal, or lining the corridors, their legs straight out ahead of them.

The nobility dare not sit even for a moment, dare not eat a bite. Each family, every ambitious counsellor and holy man, frantically reappraises their position relative to the many possible outcomes that await them. Should they have tended more respectfully to the cousin's wife, or written to the cousin praising her, imploring him to visit? Perhaps this is the critical time to find the Chief Advisor, ask if there is anything at all they can do for him. Or else should they flee, hide out in their country estates? If so, they must be quick and careful, perhaps sending servants ahead to check the way, or wait for nightfall, but by then it may be too late.

From the kitchens, spirited conversation swells, rolling through the corridors like fire. The serfs laugh loud and long at the Queen's fool who, rudderless, takes up his usual routine.

And all the while, the council sit in their chamber – the usual circle. They must act, but they are stuck. Each man can be sure only of his version of the truth. Suspicion halts every avenue explored; each remedy is sniffed for poison.

The seams are pulled tight, the threads will surely begin to break. But is it, if they're honest, not a little thrilling?

•••

THE YOUNG ATTENDANT
NO LONGER YOUNG

Years. They have moved on like the flit of a sparrow past a window.

The King's young Attendant, now old and dying, is tended by his adult daughter and her young son. It is near summer solstice, the sun hangs dutifully above the trees. He no longer knows her, or himself, or the wife with whom he spent his life, departed now a handful of years. Gone now is the memory of the profession he took up upon leaving court and the King's service – keeping books for the nobility, tracking income and outgoings, calculating dowries, seeking and recording valuations on tapestries and silver plate – though his mental arithmetic has remained remarkable. His grandson likes to test him.

In the months before he was confined to the bed he has languished in now ten days and nights, his daughter sometimes found him hovering close to the chair by the fireplace. The chair in which her mother would sit most evenings, mending or reading or staring into the flames, transfixed. *What are you looking for, Father? Are you well?* she would ask. His response came from a place she could not reach, *Quite well,* or *There was something . . .* reaching a hand out in the direction of the vacant chair.

After days of sleep, no food, a little to drink, her father brightens as the sun set. Orange light across his neck and chin. His eyes clear. He seems to see her face for the briefest moment. *Did I tell you, I must have told you, that I know the King.* Then he sleeps, promptly and deeply, the sun retreating over his mouth, nose, forehead and then off beyond the top of his head in the quiet stretch of time she remains by his side, perched on a stool he made with his own hands, flecks of dust hanging in the air between them.

For her whole life, this has been something they did not speak of. She has always known, in the way that unsayable things in a household are known but also felt, deeply, that the life of her mother and father at court, the King and household they served, were confined firmly to the realm of memory. Whatever happened changed the course of their lives in ways she could not understand. Her curiosity about the people of the court, the lives they lived, their games and dresses, paintings and jewels, would not be satisfied. She was to content herself with the views of the fields, the sheep that roamed them, and had to stop trying to paint pictures in her head.

As she grew and understood better the ways of adults, she came to realise that to speak of *that* King in company was not done. His reign was a source of great discomfort to decent people. He was the pip in the perfectly formed fruit, the rotten tooth in the otherwise healthy mouth. What kind of a King would abandon his people, leave them exposed to occupation by whoever was quickest to act? Or else, what King would be so manipulated by the Devil himself that his council had no choice but to intervene, throwing the country into a disarray that was still somehow preferable to his intolerable reign? If there had been a plan on the part of the great plotter, whoever they may have been, it was not realised. The years that followed were dark and bloody, filled with many pretenders to the throne. It is best not talked about, the country at large agrees, lest the spirit of the King is nudged from its slumber.

~

Even as a child she noticed that people looked at her father a certain way – as if he were a riddle. He was a man with a veil of sorts between himself and the world around him.

~

There was a story about the King and Queen – the ones her father had served in his youth – that children would tell each other on dark nights, the older to the younger, in the absence of their parents:

Many years after the disappearance of the King, a nobleman arrived at court claiming to have seen the bodies of the King and Queen with his own eyes, not two days ago. On the way, tired from riding, he stopped in a clearing in the forest and, when rain came, took shelter in an abandoned barn. There he found clothes strung up on a makeshift line, a burnt-out fire, creatures scurrying, empty plates and cups. Peering behind a stack of hay bales, he came upon two corpses, dressed in clothes not befitting farmers, not befitting country folk. Clothes of astonishing quality, but old and tattered. They were a long time dead, the King's head resting on the Queen's shoulder, the Queen's hand of bones, bedecked with jewels, resting on his thigh. Vermin weaved in and out of the skeletons, one even asleep inside the King's head. So, the Rat King, then. The noble-man rode off at speed, to bring people to the scene, which he never was able to locate again.

~

Since her father spoke his first words of the King, from a bed she knows he will not now get out of, he has moved backwards in his life. Behind his closed eyes he is a young man at court, muttering of nothing else in the brief interludes between sleep. For two days, he tends to the King in his memory.

The King requests

       fresh candles

   he is not to be disturbed   *fetch chamomile and nettle*

for our Lord   *he aches*

   I will keep the watch   *worry not*

he calls for me   *we were walking, that is all*

The next morning, her father wakes briefly, looking pained. He makes to sit up, his hand on the coverlet to pull it aside. *I must go to the King, he has bid me come.* She places a hand on his shoulder – not pushing him back, but firmly enough that he will not press on through the weight of it.

He looks beyond her. *I must . . .*

She stands. *As you wish, I will fetch your slippers.* She turns her back and makes slowly towards the door, where she pauses, looks back over her shoulder and sees, as expected, her father asleep once again, his mouth open to the ceiling.

Hours later, the sun is ablaze in a strip across his neck, as if rendering his head from his body. He stirs when the warmth has built on his skin. His breath is shallow in his throat.

She ventures, *Father, did you see your King?*

Her father nods in assent.

What news?

I saw him. He is gone, into another life.

III

'THE QUESTION OF PRESERVATION'

How do we know anything about history?

I posed this question to an audience of around 40 people. They were dotted and clustered among the hundred or so chairs that had been set out by the palace staff. The rows slightly too tightly packed in the beautiful room that had been designated to me when I arrived. An aisle divided the rows down the middle – a sensible approach to accommodate latecomers and people who would need to slip out, but it did give me the feeling of an officiant awaiting the arrival of the happy couple.

I continued:

When I say 'history', I don't mean things that people who are still alive can tell us about – events that happened fifteen, fifty or even a hundred years ago. I mean things that happened long enough ago that not a person on the planet today was alive to see it, nor to receive a first-hand account from those who were.

I'm not asking this rhetorically – any time I ask a question this evening, it is very much in the spirit of wanting us to have a conversation.

I gestured to my chest, then out to them, and then back at myself as I said this.

So, how do we know anything about history?

I paused.

The archivist was sitting in the front row. They blinked once, twice, slowly interlocked their fingers to form one big fist, which then rested in their lap.

Seven seconds is the amount of time you should wait for an answer before you can be quite sure no answer is coming. It can feel like forever, but it's important to create a gap that people are compelled to fill.

Four, maybe five seconds passed.

Textbooks, someone says. A teenage girl.

Textbooks, yes, I replied. *And where does the content of textbooks come from?*

A brief silence. Someone coughed. The teenage girl's face was all apology.

Records people kept at the time? Letters and diary entries?

Absolutely. We rely so much – I'd say more than anything else – on what people took the time not just to write down, but to write to each other and to themselves.

The teenage girl smiled – the affirmation embarrassed her a little, but she liked it.

What else? I asked.

A woman with a sleeping baby in a sling at her chest: *Stories and songs?*

Yes, probably our most emotive records, and not always ones that spring to mind. I waited, briefly, allowing my praise to rest on her.

Any other thoughts?

They wouldn't necessarily be accurate, but I suppose art . . . So, paintings and tapestries? This from a youngish man in the second row, impeccably dressed in black, dazzling rings on his fingers, painted black nails.

Yes, very good, and I'm glad you've mentioned accuracy. You're making my job very easy for me. Can you say more about what you mean when you say they might not be accurate?

Well, I guess I mean they might be more like propaganda, presenting a version of events, rather than what actually happened. More likely to glorify or exaggerate, or to make someone seem really evil.

That's true, and we're right to approach all records with an amount of scepticism, but even propaganda, or flattery or mythologising or whatever we want to call it, they can all tell us something really valuable about the events, about the times and the mood of those times, and often about what followed. For example, in the archives of this palace, I found a poem which praised a King for his victory in battle. It goes something like this: the King's troops were outnumbered, but in their bravery they pushed back foreign invaders, who retreated like scolded dogs, and the land was theirs once again. Those fallen are likened to lions. By the end of the poem the battle-weary men are bathing in the clear waters of a stream, singing songs to the glory of the King. But the facts are very different – numerous sources confirm that the battle was long, drawn out, and that the King himself overruled the sage advice of his council to make ill-advised decisions which lost them many lives. Why then? Why then the poem?

Again, I waited.

The King paid someone to write it? To change history in his favour?

Very possible, I said.

The poet wanted something from the King – maybe he thought it would secure him favour or a position at court? Didn't sycophants or favourites often get rewarded? So, like a trade – poem for status.

Again, could be.

Again, the young man with the rings: *Maybe it was a necessary act of propaganda. Imagine how furious the families of the dead soldiers would have been if they knew they didn't need to die – that the fault lay with the King alone.*

And why a poem? I asked.

More memorable, he said, *more persuasive.*

I nodded slowly. *And which of you is right?*

I paused to sip some water and let the audience shuffle. I had learnt a little drama from the archivist.

OK, that question perhaps was rhetorical. Of course you all know that we probably have no way of knowing who is right. Maybe none of you, and perhaps also all of you, partially. Now, before I release you to explore the many rooms of this incredible palace, I want to talk to you a bit about the power of records. Records, and also what we can learn from their gaps. Here is an example that has nothing directly to do with the building we're all sitting in now, and then I'll come to the inspiration behind my scene setting for this project.

Here is something we know because of records: there were 286 types of apple growing and available in Italy in the 1800s. And we know this only because a man named Garnier Valletti rendered in resin or wax a replica of every single variety, and that collection now sits behind glass, numbered and named, in the Museo della Frutta in Turin. We do not know it because those 286 types of apple still exist today. They do not. Nor do we know it because any person who had the pleasure to sit and eat 286 apples – in the unlikely event that they should have ever existed in the first place – is still alive to share those details with us. We have access to this knowledge only because it was meticulously recorded. Their appearance, firmness to touch, colour, size, shape, structure of flesh and propensity for browning in the open air. Their blossom, which bees liked to visit, the pitch of the thud they made when they fell to the grass, rolled in the dew, were hollowed by caterpillars. These facts, recorded clearly, legibly, happened to survive.

Until recently, the replica fruits were scattered around the Royal Station of Agricultural Chemistry, abandoned for almost a hundred years, wrapped in boxes and stored on shelves. There was so much material that it took ten years to get the museum ready for opening. And so, we have this incredible, detailed record of things that once existed, all thanks to Garnier Valletti. The skins of the apples shine as if caught in the light, they have real stalks, blemishes. He used powdered wool to capture the skin of peaches and apricots, and finely crushed white stone on the grapes, having moved to other fruit once the apples were all accounted for. But tell me, what does this incredible feat of record keeping not tell us?

The same teenage girl: *What they tasted like?*

Exactly. And what are apples for if not eating? This person tried so hard to immortalise each apple, and they have, but of course, in another sense, they haven't at all. A resin model is only a part of the story – we aren't actually encountering an apple. It's like being haunted by the ghost of a person you never met. It's like taxidermy. Why then? Why do you think he did it?

It might have been a commission, for a school of botany or something? ventured an elderly man I hadn't noticed until he spoke.

That would be as good an explanation as any. And it would tell us about the interests and fashions of study of the time. But what if it wasn't a commission? What then?

Someone in the back row: *Maybe he just really loved doing it – maybe it was an art form to him.*

Sure – what's the difference between painting apples and making models of apples? No one questions why painters create nude after nude, or myth after myth on the canvas. It's a fair point.

Someone else: *Maybe he was just obsessed with apples, like when people fill their house with collectible figurines in boxes.*

Again, possible. Complete devotion.

Then the archivist, who could not help themselves: *To make us confront, one day, what we have lost.*

I let this comment hang in the air, allowing time for the weight of its perfection to settle on everyone's shoulders.

Silence.

~

The night before this lecture, as I ate my dinner – a dinner which, incidentally, I found myself enjoying in a way I had not for weeks – I thought of the archivist. As I often did: on my way home or to the palace, while at home, and in between other places. Earlier that day we had spoken about their work, how they came to find themselves in this strange and dusty corner of history. A school trip – the class lining up to peer into the pages of a very old book. The very old book being held open by the perfectly whitely gloved hand of its keeper. The other students commented on the paper, how stained and frail, or on the cover, how ornate, or else they were not interested at all; not falling silent, even for a moment, or stopping to really look. When it came to the archivist's turn, they stopped, they looked into the pages and felt they had fallen into them – the voices on the page were alive and real, moving in, through and out of their ears, as if conducting a most efficient and welcome possession. The archivist was holding up the line, had to be moved along by the teacher, but not before looking up beyond those gloved hands, to the arms, shoulders, neck and then face of the protector of this book. Eye contact, immediate recognition. As they told me this story, I watched the colour rise beyond the open top button of their shirt, and bloom onto their neck.

Since the archivist told me this story, I had run it over in my mind. I imagined that it happened at exactly the moment I squeezed the hollow grape in the furniture superstore. The moment the world rotated a degree for us both, allowing us in through a thin crack and beyond to a new, sparsely inhabited place. Where before, alone in my house, I had felt boxed in – upon the door closing behind me, sealed off discretely from the world – I now imagined a thread tethering me to what lay beyond.

~

I nodded to a member of the office staff, stationed by the light switches, who promptly flicked them up in two neat movements. Darkness, then the light from the projector on my desk, which I summoned with a single press of a button. The King's ledger entry, his great humiliation, emblazoned on the wooden panelling behind me.

I invited the audience to read. I gave them four minutes – plenty of time, I estimated, for two reads at least.

The beauty of records, I said, is that they can be remade in our minds. They are forever morphing. At least, they should be. There is a very great danger, I believe, in assuming that because something is set in ink (or stone, or paint, or silk, or replica food for that matter) and has been stored in the dark for years, that it cannot be retrieved, blown free of dust, held to the light. No record-maker should have the last say, no record should be final.

When you leave this room and begin your tour of the palace, you are entering the world of this King – I pointed to the projection on the wall – *who lived here some hundreds of years ago. But it is not just any day in his world – it is the day of his disappearance. His, along with his Queen's. The sun has been up for two or three hours, and a sense of quiet panic is starting to spread through the court, along with many theories about what has happened and where they have gone.*

I warn you now that there are no answers to these questions.

His great gift to us – or at least it has been a gift to me – is the very lack of an ending, that could drive a historian mad. What a great – pardon my language – 'fuck you' to everyone who tries to manhandle ambiguity into order, to knock out the air. To the people that have since pinned him down so cruelly and unambiguously on this page. To the notion that one thing leads to another and then another and then done. To the idea that we owe anyone the answers they seek – for they are theirs alone to find.

I felt some emotion rising in my throat. I swallowed and waited. I looked again at the archivist's hands, still balled into a fist, and thought of them only hours ago rearranging a bowl of replica apples as if they were precious eggs. It had become clear to me as I began to assemble the scenes – the kind of pure clarity that comes without the need for thinking – that the archivist must be a part of it. I told them that for every piece I positioned, every decision I made, they should make an opposing or concurrent one. Knowing what they did about my particular way of working, they expressed hesitation, which I understood. Would they not be meddling? What if they made a decision I disagreed with? The point, though, I said, the whole point was that I needed a safeguard against certainty – I could not be permitted to create a definitive story for my King, setting him firmly in a history bent to my desires.

You will start in the kitchens and end in the great hall. I want you to remember what has been recorded of him, what you have just read, and I ask that you let this person expand into the rooms, into the air around you. Listen for everything and, above all, pay attention.

The doors at the back of the room were opened then, and the audience began to leave. I watched them shuffle out, file down the corridor, turn left, and head down into the kitchens. It was all waiting – perfect and in position. I envied them.

THE KITCHENS

Along the left side of the room, dinner is lined up in huge quantities for the people of the court. Many dark loaves on wooden boards, poached salmon and trout on platters, pies of fruit and meat with latticed tops, joints of ham with an almost boastful glisten, large bowls of stew, dark and shining. The food is laid out in blocks – stew follows meat follows pies follows fish follows the mounds of bread – to be retrieved one by one for distribution among the court's many apartments and rooms.

On the central table are arranged all manner of kitchen items – chopping boards, knives, rolling pins, grinding stones, cleavers, a single silver spoon, face-down, as if ashamed. Discarded offcuts of vegetables – elaborate carrot tops, potato peelings, the hairy bases of swedes. Mutton bones, stripped clean and brilliant white, small morsels of cheese with discernible human toothmarks. Rolled-out pastry with shapes cut out by hand – a rooster, a lion and a peacock, leaves, the petals of bear's breeches, three swans.

Preparation has been abandoned: a carrot half cut and the knife beside it, a bowl half full of stew, the ladle resting against its edge.

In the fire is a pig on a spit, its head removed and placed on a small butchery block in the far corner of the room. In the pig's mouth is a whole quince – it wears a garland of white flowers and gleams like a toffee apple. Its body, predictably impaled through the centre of the neck at one end and the arse at the other, appears to hover above the fire. Its back legs have been pinned to its side and its front legs are stretched out ahead of it, as if it is reaching across the room for its own head.

Along the right side of the room, a long table is adorned with the kitchen's finest silver plates – etched with seashells and pinecones. All immaculate, ornate, empty.

THE QUEEN'S PARLOUR

Two low tapestried chairs are angled towards one another conspiratorially. Between them sits a small round table, upon which is placed an open book, face-down. The book has no title on the cover or the spine. It is jacketed in a rich blue leather. On the same table rests an unfinished embroidery: a woman in a long blue gown stands barefoot on grass, which is dotted with pink flowers. Her head is uncovered and she is hitching her skirt ever so slightly to reveal one delicate foot. Her other hand rests on the trunk of an orange tree, which sits at the embroidery's centre, its crown crowded with emerald leaves, the fruits vivid and constellating. On the tree's other side is a second hand, in perfect symmetry with the other, the shirt cuff of a man, and the beginnings of his arm, also clothed in blue. The arm stops at the elbow, from where the blue thread cuts across the fabric, taut in the frame, and disappears over the edge of the table. On closer inspection, the thread is weighted down by the needle, still threaded, which hangs a few centimetres from the floor, occasionally rocked by otherwise imperceptible movements in the air.

From an angle only afforded by standing by the largest window, which looks out over an expansive stretch of lawn bordered by mulberry trees, four screwed-up balls of parchment can be seen lying discarded beneath the shadow of the bed, as if thrown.

At a small desk, a quill sits broken in the inkwell, the tip submerged. On a blank sheet of parchment has been placed the dry stem and flower of a lavender plant.

AN ATTENDANT'S QUARTERS

On a desk, which also serves as a table for taking all meals and a surface upon which to rest your head during brief breaks between shifts, as well as the place to leave anything you do not want to forget to take from the room with you, being as it is situated beside the door – on that desk has been placed a pile of papers, thick as a good wedge of bread, utterly out of place, tied with string. On top of the wedge of papers is a folded letter – you cannot make out the writing inside even if you hold it up to the candlelight, which you cannot do – closed by the King's seal.

The bed is unmade, the simple hemp coverlet thrown off on one side and crumpled on the other. The pillows still have the impressions of the room's occupants in them – indents where the fabric has worn thin – and their upper inner corners lean towards one another, almost inquisitively, almost as foreheads touching.

Also on the desk, which serves as a table and a resting spot and a reminder, is a small brown bottle, and a glass, two-thirds full. The cork stopper is present and correct. Finally, on a dull pewter plate is a small chewet, quartered. Half of the pie remains upright, one quarter lies on its back, and the remaining quarter is gone. The marbling of the meat brings to mind exactly that – marble, pink and white.

THE MEDICAL PARAPHERNALIA
AND PRACTICES OF THE TIME

The table of the Assistant to the Royal Physician: kept immaculate.

A leather tool bag, unravelled, revealing an awl, a scalpel, tweezers, three knives, two pairs of scissors, a bone saw, a set of silver spoons engraved with tiny motifs of aloe vera, saffron, hemlock, henbane, liquorice, coriander, mint and wormwood.

Dark blue and brown glass bottles in a line – oils and ointments for muscle ache, toothache, festering wounds.

One missing – betrayed by a long-dried ring of oil.

THE KING'S CHAMBERS

The King's bedroom is in perfect order – the chair pushed under the desk, the candles startlingly upright, burnt down a third. Peeking from the pages of a book of prayers is a pressed copper birch leaf, used to mark the page.

The bed is made, the trunk at its foot is closed.

A great stack of papers sits in the grate, singed at the edges, and the bottom of the pile burnt to ash, the weight of the pages having eventually extinguished the unreplenished fire. Visible on the top sheet are the words WARRANT TO EXECUTE – the name that followed has been taken by the flames. The space for the King's signature and seal is blank. To the left of the fire, at the edge of the hearth, is a small, empty pewter dish.

The fruit bowl on the table is resplendent with apples, pomegranates and pears. They are piled into a pleasing mound, absolute abundance – with what appears to be a single empty space. Phantom fruit.

A tankard sits on the stone sill of a window that looks out over the rose garden.

Of the two large wardrobes, one is closed and one is open a fraction; just visible in the gap's darkness is a cloak of purple silk.

An apple, green and blush pink, rests in the corner of the room, mostly masked by the hem of the curtain.

AN ELABORATE FEAST SCENE
IN THE GREAT HALL

There is a feast on the long central table, as there always must be, but it is pared back – each dish complementary to another and served in restrained quantities. A plate of perfectly almond-shaped almond biscuits with specks of black pepper. Cinnamon cakes the size of a single bite. A single joint of ham wrapped in wilted vine leaves and topped with gleaming slices of orange. A trio of pies – all concealing their insides. One whole salmon, poached, head and tail still intact. A queue of lemon slices at its belly. Bread, cheese, one roasted leg of chicken, a jelly of many colours in the shape of a rose.

Three places set with silver plates and fine goblets, upon whose rims the grease of three mouths is visible, in the right light. Two jugs – one ceramic and one pewter – holding beer and wine. Taper candles in the sconces on the walls, running the length of the table and clustered in higher concentration at the dining end. Along the back wall, the pewter plates of the servants, adorned with scraps of bread and ham, form a semi-orderly line.

The place at the head of the table is positioned directly opposite the view out onto a cluster of beech trees, their leaves meandering from russet to golden yellow.

At one window – in the very darkest corner – a glow. A glow of orange that seems to flicker, to swell and retreat, to cast its dubious light across the adjacent walls.

EPILOGUE

The palace, predictably, had thoughts about the somewhat un-
orthodox approach I had taken. They weren't unhappy per se, but
we talked it through in a special meeting I was invited to attend, I
assume to explain myself. They had some things to say. They felt
the research period had been disproportionately long and resulted
in a rushed completion ahead of the big weekend, which caused
unnecessary stress for the team. Drafting in the archivist so late
in the process had also taken them away from their regular work,
reducing the time they had to prepare for their own events. I wished
keenly then that the archivist were in the room with me to fight my
corner, to explain why it had to be that way. And the needle at the
end of the blue thread, suspended from the table (for example) –
what exactly was the point? Who would realistically see it and, if
they did, ascribe to it any meaning? Would my time not have been
better spent perhaps arranging some pink diamond-shaped sugar
sweets on a small plate, or draping a fine brocade skirt over the back
of a chair? Things people could easily see and understand. Things
people *want* to see. Someone would have noticed it, the thread,

and it could have been the catalyst for all sorts of possibilities in their mind – this was my response, and even as it came out of my mouth I knew it wasn't compelling. Or rather: wouldn't be compelling to them. I thought of the archivist's reaction to the King's chambers after I made my final adjustments – their eyes shooting from the fruit bowl to the cloak, to the fireplace and then the apple – and I knew it was perfect. Take the purple cloak, the palace staff went on, an original medieval cloak with a price tag to match, and it was visible through the smallest crack in the wardrobe door. The person who had been speaking the most levelled this grievance, then exhaled slowly and at length. I didn't have much else to offer to the conversation.

Before I left – while I was opening the door, in fact – I turned and asked if I might take those items I had purchased to make the scenes, in exchange for a reduction in my fee. I did it like that, as if it occurred to me only as I was leaving, but the truth is I'd thought about little else since the project had ended. As it happened, the palace had just secured a booking for a film for the following spring – they would be closed to the public for at least half of the year. They had no real need for the scenes beyond the anniversary celebrations, which would wrap up at the end of the month. They said there was no sense in everything just sitting in boxes in storage – they would forward everything on to me when the scenes were dismantled. I sensed they resented this agreement, which perhaps felt a little too close to doing me a favour. We agreed a price.

I'm glad my work got you what you needed, in the end. My parting shot.

~

My most pervasive dream, for at least the last couple of years, was not exactly troubling, more disconcerting. Time and again, I found myself, by unexplained mechanisms, cross-legged in a Perspex box. The box is tied to a rope, which lowers me into various bodies of water – usually deep and dark – and raises me from them again just at the point where I begin to fear I will never again see the sky.

But I have not had that dream since the day I met the archivist. I rarely allow myself to ascribe meaning, given as we all are to dropping logic at the earliest opportunity in favour of magical thinking, but in this case I find I have to concede.

~

Four weeks later, the boxes arrived. They were delivered to me on a Friday afternoon in light rain. I immediately set to work removing the items, which to the palace's credit had been wrapped very carefully, and decanted them onto the chairs surrounding my dining table, and then onto the floor when the chairs were full. I flattened each box when it was empty and made a stack of them.

I have to be honest. Since I left the palace on that Sunday evening, leaving the public to their tour and their imaginings, I have felt unmoored. I have turned a few different words over in my mind, and unmoored is the best I can do. I am still somewhat tethered to the King, but as a parent who loses their child in the supermarket might feel for the first few seconds, before the real panic sets in. Otherwise, floating about in this life, in this place, finding myself again queasy to be at home in the quiet, in the dark – though certainly less than before. The dining table a glowering vacancy still, but in the middle a silver fork – permitted for use by the King alone – with a single pomegranate seed impaled on the left prong. It would have been too great a risk to take nothing before that final meeting.

But now: ten apples, ten pears, five pomegranates, grapes of green and red. A chewet (all four quarters) as well as a complete version I ended up not making use of, hunks of bread, three simple wooden plates, five engraved silver platters. Eight dark loaves of bread, many poached trout, altogether at least twenty-five pies of varying sizes, shapes and decoration, six joints of ham, around ten roasted chickens or chicken legs, bowls with stews of carrots and mutton suspended in resin. Miscellaneous hunks of bread, biscuits. Slices of orange, a whole salmon with head and tail, slices of lemon. When the salmon had first arrived at the palace I had marvelled at the detail of not only the fins, but the gills too, with their just-visible strip of scarlet. I marvelled once again. An array of cheeses – I was once again struck by the faithfulness of their renderings. One ceramic jug, one pewter mug, the tankard that had belonged to the King. In a larger rectangular box, the pig – spit dutifully removed, the head temporarily reunited with the torso, the quince a glowing orb in the corner. In a final box: the pile of singed papers, the stack of parchments tied with string, the letter with the King's wax seal, the set of glass medicine bottles in blue and brown glass, the seven gilded candlesticks, the unfinished embroidery in its ring.

The palace had provided so much in the way of furniture, accessories and other paraphernalia from their own stock and stores (and, understandably, they kept the purple cloak for future exhibitions) that I had no hope of recreating the scenes exactly, and nor did I want to. I needed only extract their spirit.

I selected the two most compelling candlesticks and set them on the dining table, inserted tapered beeswax candles. To their left I placed the King's book, now missing its birch leaf. Where had it fallen and settled? I wondered. In the garden, I snipped a leaf from the bay tree and used that to mark the same page as before. A page I knew well. I arranged the part-burnt stack of papers in the grate of my fire, and completed it with the pewter dish, into which I placed a small piece of sliced ham. I had purchased an original bowl, appropriate for the era – wooden, engraved with a repeating chain-link pattern – at not inconsiderable cost. Into it went the pears, the pomegranates, the apples, adorned at one edge by a bunch of green grapes. This time, the mound of apples would be complete, but I placed the final piece on the corner of the table, in readiness for the archivist doing the honours.

I tried the tankard in various places – the shelf by the back door, an occasional table at the bottom of the stairs by the porch where I tend to leave my car keys, the coffee table that looks out onto my front garden, then the mantelpiece in the kitchen, with a view onto the back garden, which is where it ultimately felt best placed. It looked almost luminous in the grey-lilac late-afternoon light.

I returned to the table, stepping over the bisected pig, and took a seat. I moved the items in fractions, encouraging them to speak to one another, until they felt settled. The abandoned embroidery found its way onto my lap, into my hands, and I started once again at the arm of the King.

ACKNOWLEDGEMENTS

All my thanks and gratitude, which are impossible to capture adequately in words, to early readers of this manuscript: Charlotte Adlard, Crispin Best, A K Blakemore and Amy Key, you shaped MWFTK into the book it is now and I am so grateful. To dear friends who, over many years, have encouraged, challenged, celebrated, made me think in new ways – Natasha Bloor, Eli Goldstone, Alex MacDonald, Richard Scott, Laura Webb, Bryony White and Jane Yeh. I love you all. To my cats Patsy and Otter, who can't read but bring me joy every day, and to Amy Key, again, for everything. To Ross for our life, which makes me so happy, and to my family (my mum and dad, and my brother Mark, plus sprawling networks of extended and not-quite family) for the constancy of their love, care and interest.

Thank you to my agent Seren Adams for shepherding this project, to the team at Granta for their careful handling of it, and to my editor Dan Bird for asking all the questions that needed to be answered. I am also incredibly grateful to have received a Society of Authors' Foundation grant, which supported the writing of this book.